DAVID GRACE

Three of Blood

Book One | Children of the Realms

First edition

This book was professionally typeset on Reedsy.
Find out more at reedsy.com

Contents

One

Larissa

Larissa stood at the bottom of the stairs; her hands pressed to the fabric of her white linen dress. She tried to straighten the wrinkles, but the fabric wouldn't cooperate. It felt too tight around her chest, like the air had turned heavy, suffocating. The faint clink of the deadbolt slipping into place echoed behind her, sharp in the quiet of the morning.

She closed her eyes, watching the vision play out once more: fallen maple leaves swirling across the sidewalk, mixing with the city's grime, as they drifted toward the street. The gold sedan passed by, turning the corner. The red truck honking just as the young man sprinted across the road. She opened her eyes and watched the same gold sedan turn the corner, the familiar sequence unfolding.

Her dad's voice broke through her thoughts, warm and casual. "Ready for school, kiddo?" He handed her the bag, a soft smile on his face as he passed, heading down the stairs. Larissa forced a smile in return, the weight of the moment pressing down on her.

"Yeah," she muttered, following him onto the sidewalk, the red truck honking in the distance, as she watched the young man sprint across the road.

"Everything okay, Lari?"

Larissa looked up, swallowing the knot in her throat. She knew there was no changing this. Not today. Not ever. She had tried, so many times. Her heart felt like it was in a vise, tightening with every step.

"Yeah, everything's fine," she said, the lie slipped out before she could stop it. "For a second, I thought I forgot my homework, but I'm pretty sure I put it in my bag after dinner." She tried to smile, but it felt wrong, hollow. Her father chuckled, linking their arms together.

"Wanna check to make sure?"

"No, that's okay. Homework or not, I always pass." She offered a halfhearted shrug, trying to mask the dread creeping in.

He ruffled her hair. "I know you do, my smart girl."

The two of them continued to walk, her dad's steps steady, but Larissa's pace had slowed. She could feel the tears welling up, the sting at the back of her eyes. This moment—it never got easier. She had lived it many times, each time feeling the same, each time somehow more suffocating than the last.

Her dad tugged gently on her arm, drawing her attention to the corner ahead. Her heart raced.

"Excited for game night tonight?" he asked, his voice light, normal.

Larissa's stomach twisted. She could hardly breathe, let alone muster excitement for a night that would never happen. "Hey, Dad?" she said, her voice barely above a whisper.

"Yeah?"

"You know that I love you, right?"

They turned the corner, and for the briefest moment, the world felt like it was spinning in slow motion. The white van was coming—hurtling toward them. Her pulse quickened, the cold weight of inevitability pressing in.

"Of course I do," her dad said, his brow furrowing with concern. "I love you too, kiddo. Are you sure everything's okay?"

Larissa nodded, swallowing the lump in her throat. "Yeah, everything's fine." But her voice was thin, fragile, as if she was already losing control.

The sound of tires screeching tore through the air, and she saw it—the van veering off the road, heading straight for them. Her father's head snapped toward the sound, his instincts kicking in. Without thinking, he shoved her away, his body moving toward the van with sudden desperation.

Larissa closed her eyes, shutting out the horror she already knew was coming.

She didn't need to see it. She'd already seen it too many times.

The sickening crunch of metal and bone echoed in her mind, and the air around her felt thick and suffocating. When she opened her eyes again, the vision was the same. Three tulips—broken and scattered on the ground—lay in front of her. The flowers had broken from the impact of her backpack. She picked them up slowly, her fingers numb as she clutched them in her hand.

She stumbled toward the garden gate, the iron cold beneath her fingertips. The noise from the crash faded into a dull hum, as though the world had slowed down, leaving her in this quiet, empty space. She walked into the garden, toward the swing beneath the oak tree, her footsteps heavy and deliberate. A bird flew in front of her landing on a bush in front of some very large windows.

Larissa reached the swing, dropped her backpack off her shoulder without any concern. She turned her body away from the swing and sat down. As she drew herself back and forth with her heels on the ground, she tried to hold it together. Tears were continuous down both her cheeks. Her only comfort: this was the end of her vision. From here she no longer knew what would happen. In that she found a bit of peace.

The bird squawked and as Larissa turned towards the noise, she could see through the large windows a woman running down the hallway. Her head numb, she starred blankly through the windows. An old lady was starring back at her, she waved at Larissa. Larissa raised a hand, a weak, automatic gesture, though it felt out of place, almost surreal.

The gate creaked as it opened, and Larissa's gaze shifted toward the approaching figure. A police officer, his uniform crisp against the morning light, moved slowly toward her. He said something—her mind couldn't focus on the words. It didn't matter. All that mattered was that her dad was gone.

She was alone.

Without a word, she stood, her legs unsteady beneath her. She dropped the flowers on the swing, grabbed her backpack, and followed the officer out of the garden. The bird followed as well.

Two

The Dream

The girl lay motionless on the ground, her once-white linen dress stained with dirt, concrete dust, and sweat. Her long, dark hair, resembling the wet fur of a Chesapeake Bay retriever, clung to her skin in thick strands, some matted against her cheek, forming a grimy crust. The light above swayed like a pendulum, casting long shadows across her body, while the evidence of new scratches—raw and jagged—marked her arms and hands as the light flickered.

Kate knelt beside the lifeless figure, feeling the tension in the air, an electric, fragile stillness that contrasted sharply with the frantic energy of the living child beside her. Across from Kate knelt a second girl, her face smeared with dirt, except for two clean streaks where tears had carved their path. Her hair, streaked with sunlight, stuck out in wild directions, as if each strand had a mind of its own.

The girl's breath came in frantic gasps, and her body shook as she rocked back and forth. She clutched Kate's hands and forced them down onto the dead girl's chest. "Please! Save her!" she cried, her voice raw with desperation. "Save her!" Over and over, the words repeated in a litany, her face twisted with fear.

Kate's heart pounded as she tried to pull her hands away, but the little girl's grip was firm, unyielding. Kate sobbed; the words caught in her throat. "I can't! I can't!" She pulled her hands back, but the girl's hold didn't loosen. It was only when the child's tiny fingers finally released that Kate's hands were free, and the girl's head *dropped back to rest against the lifeless body. The child had given up.*

"I can't..." Kate whispered, but no one heard.

Kate jolted awake, her scream a raw echo in the dark. She thrashed her head against the pillow, kicking the covers off as the sweat soaked through her nightshirt. "Dammit, Dad heard that," she muttered under her breath. She wiped the sweat from her face, pretending to settle into the bed, her eyes closing as she waited.

A moment later, the door crashed open. Her father, misjudging the distance in the dark, collided with the side of the bed, his voice urgent. "Kate! Wake up!"

With a groan, Kate sat up in bed, already feeling the familiar weight of exhaustion. Her father, too emotional for his own good, threw his arms around her neck. At twenty years old, this was ridiculous. She was too old for this kind of thing, and yet, it had happened five nights in a row. The nightmare clung to her like a shadow, and she couldn't stop screaming.

The thought made her cringe, her skin burning with embarrassment. She wasn't a child anymore. She was in her twenties, for god's sake, and yet here she was, needing her dad to comfort her after a bad dream.

"Hey," she mumbled, awkwardly pulling away from his embrace. "Did you even knock?"

Her father grinned sheepishly. "Well, I figured with all the screaming, you might need some help." He scooped up her hand, clearly not buying her tough-girl act.

"Dad," she said, trying to sound firm, though it came out more like a plea. "I'm twenty. You can't just keep barging in every time I have a bad dream."

He raised an eyebrow. "Was it the girls again?"

Kate shifted uncomfortably, refusing to meet his gaze. He always asked, but she could never bring herself to tell him. Not about the little girl who kept dying in her arms, night after night. Not about the feeling of helplessness that twisted her gut every time she saw the girl's tear-streaked face.

"No..." Kate muttered, turning away. "It was... spiders." She couldn't look him in the eyes, and as soon as the words left her mouth, she felt like a fraud.

A grown woman lying to her dad about nightmares? Pathetic.

Her dad's gaze softened. "Spiders, huh?" He chuckled, squeezing her hand before releasing it. "Well, as long as you're okay…?"

Kate nodded, but the thought of those little hands gripping hers, of the lifeless body, of the hopelessness, still haunted her.

Her dad stood, his knees creaking as he pushed himself up. She couldn't help but notice the wear in his movements—the way he shifted his weight before stepping toward the door.

"Good night, Kate," he said, his voice warm but tinged with a hint of sadness, like he knew how much of a child she still was inside.

"Hey, Dad?" Kate called, and he paused, looking back at her with a knowing smile.

"Yes, sweetie?"

"Thanks, Dad." She returned his grin, feeling a little less ridiculous now.

"Good night, baby," he said softly.

"And hey, maybe ice those knees when you get the chance." She couldn't resist the urge to tease him.

He laughed, pulling the door closed behind him.

Kate sank back onto the bed, exhaling sharply. The dream was already creeping back into her mind. The little girl pleading with her—it was all she could think about. Six nights in a row. Each time, it played the same. Every night, the same hopelessness. The image was inked into her conscience, a tattoo she couldn't scrub off, no matter how hard she tried.

The exhaustion weighed heavily on her, but she couldn't sleep. She threw herself out of bed, stretching her arms above her head. The clanking of dishes drifted up from the kitchen, and she smiled. Her dad would be making breakfast—probably hot chocolate with marshmallows piled high, just the way she liked it.

As she moved toward the bathroom, the dream returned, vivid in her mind. She sighed, wondering why it had to be kids. And death.

It was Tuesday, Kate's day for coffee. As she turned the key to the door, balancing a backpack over her left shoulder, her purse over her right, and four iced venti non-fat lattes tightly shoved into a drink carrier in her right hand, she couldn't help but ponder the fascination with making only one trip. Was it laziness, or just an obsessive need to save time? Either way, every Tuesday morning she found herself in this precarious balancing act, trying to make it through the industrial doors. She could have just made two trips.

The straps of her backpack slid to her forearm, and she sighed. "Why don't I just make two trips?" she muttered to herself, laughing a little. She knew better but did it anyway.

She made it through the door, a sense of accomplishment bubbling up inside. Another successful one-trip morning. Today, she decided, was her lucky day. Bad dreams be damned.

She started her morning routine, placing the drinks on the break room table and stashing her bag in her locker. After running a quick comb through her hair, she checked herself in the mirror. Yep, today was going to be a good day.

Grabbing two of the drinks, she headed down the hall to the front waiting area. The hallway always calmed her. One side was lined with private therapy rooms, while the other was floor-to-ceiling glass, offering a view of the courtyard. A black bird with red feathers and a purple band around its neck, flew by catching her eye. As she stood, holding a drink in each hand, she watched the bird swoop down, then back up to its branch. She has seen this very same bird every day for the last week. She felt her morning's anxiousness slowly begin to seep away.

It was a good day.

The bird continued its flight, swooping back and forth between the branches of the giant oak tree in the middle of the courtyard, and around the lonely swing that hung from one of the branches. Kate wondered, as she had many times before, why a swing was on that tree. She couldn't remember ever seeing anyone using it.

She made her way down the hall, glancing into the main therapy room. Mrs. Clark and Carol were already at work with their first patients. Kate felt a wave of affection for both women—Mrs. Clark, the owner, who had become like a second mother to her, and Carol, her best friend since high school.

Kate often marveled at how Mrs. Clark stayed so fit. At least fifty-five, but she wouldn't say for sure, Mrs. Clark could maneuver the largest of patients all day long and still be up for a round of tennis. Kate was exhausted just thinking about it.

Oh crap, it was Tuesday. Mrs. Clark was wearing purple. Kate checked her outfit. Yep, purple. They always coordinated, and Tuesday was purple. Not that Mrs. Clark would have mentioned it if she hadn't. Carol and Kate could do no wrong in her eyes.

She couldn't wait to talk to Carol about the dream. Carol was the perfect mix of caring and sassiness, always making Kate feel safe, like they could face anything together.

Carol caught Kate staring at her and jogged over to an exercise ball, her ponytail bouncing with each step. She gave it a kick in Kate's direction, and Kate intercepted it with a quick, practiced kick back into place.

Back to the front reception area. She walked behind the desk, passing Tina sitting at her station.

"Good morning, Tina," Kate greeted, handing her one of the drinks.

"Oh, I need this!" Tina said, grabbing the drink with one hand while also reaching for some paperwork from the printer.

"One drink down, one to go," Kate thought, making her way to the mini-fridge in the therapy room where they kept the cold packs. There was a dedicated spot on the top shelf just for Mrs. Clark's daily coffee fix. Kate loved working here. Carol's and her lattes could wait a little longer.

Drink delivered, she glanced at the clock. She had a few minutes before her first patient arrived. Absently, she walked over to the cleaning supply station, picking up a spray bottle and towel.

Her gaze drifted to Carol, who was working on Sherman. He'd been her Tuesday morning client for six weeks, and by the sweat on his forehead, it was clear he wasn't keeping up with his at-home exercises.

Kate began wiping down the table as she glanced over at Carol. Her best friend was clearly ready for their morning chat. Kate spoke first.

"I had THE dream again."

Carol looked up, eyebrows raised. "Again? Is that five nights in a row?"

"Six. And, of course, Dad came to the rescue," Kate replied, rubbing her forehead.

"I love your dad. He's so…" Carol started.

Kate cut her off. "Don't even say it," she warned, groaning. Carol always teased her about how attractive she thought Kate's dad was.

Carol just smiled, going about her work. She raised Sherman's leg and applied some tension. He let out a small groan. Carol, ever the one to push Kate's buttons, started in again.

"Was it the same? The two girls, and you didn't help them?"

"Not Didn't, I can't! Yes, the same," Kate muttered, fighting the rising anxiety. Carol loved pushing her buttons, and Kate secretly loved that about her—except when it made her feel like a child.

"Don't you think that's weird? Six days in a row?" Carol pressed, ignoring Kate's exasperated sigh.

The front door chimed, signaling the arrival of Kate's first patient.

"Yeah, I'm completely done with it," Kate said, walking to put the cleaning supplies away. "I'll talk to you a bit."

"Well, maybe tonight you'll save her?" Carol teased, but Kate could only give her a quick glare over her shoulder.

Kate walked to the reception desk, where Mrs. Peterson was already seated with a tin on her lap.

"Please let it be lemon bars," Kate thought as she greeted Mrs. Peterson.

"Good morning, Mrs. Peterson. Ready to get started?"

"Of course, dear. I promised Helen I'd have lunch with her, so I don't want to be late."

Mrs. Peterson handed Kate the tin, and she eagerly opened it before her patient had even finished speaking. "Lemon bars! You shouldn't spoil me like this," Kate said, shoving one into her mouth.

"I could never show up empty-handed. You've helped me so much," Mrs. Peterson said warmly.

Kate gave her a smile and placed the tin on the back table in the reception area. Mrs. Peterson had already started down the hall; Kate followed her down towards the last private room.

As they walked, Kate caught a glimpse of Carol heading for the reception desk and shot her a disapproving look, quickly followed by a grin. There would be half as many lemon bars when she returned.

She didn't know what she'd do without Carol. They'd been inseparable since Carol moved to town in ninth grade. They shared everything—hopes, dreams, and even lemon bars. After high school, they had both applied to the same college and gone into physical therapy. The new therapy center that had opened took both of them in as interns. It had worked out perfectly. Mrs. Clark had already offered them full-time positions as soon as they graduated.

"I really love this new facility," Mrs. Peterson said, breaking Kate's train of thought.

"It's a great place to work," Kate agreed, though her mind was only half on the conversation as she assessed Mrs. Peterson's hips as they moved.

They stopped as Mrs. Peterson paused in front of the windows, admiring the flowers in the courtyard as she often did. "What a beautiful white linen dress. I had one just like it when I was a little girl."

Kate turned to follow her gaze and froze. "What the hell?" she whispered.

The girl from her dream was sitting on the swing, holding flowers.

Kate quickly put her hand over her mouth. The girl looked exactly as she had in the dream—same dress, same disheveled hair, except she was alive.

"Mrs. Peterson, can you excuse me for a minute?" Kate didn't wait for a response before she sprinted down the hall, her heart pounding in her chest.

"Carol!" she called in a voice that was far too loud and frantic for the calm she was trying to project.

Carol and Bob both turned, startled. Carol immediately began walking toward her, her expression one of concern. Bob returned to his biking.

"What's wrong? You look like you've seen a ghost."

"Come with me. You're not going to believe this." Kate couldn't slow her heart rate as she jogged down the hall, Carol right behind her.

"There! In the garden!" Kate pointed frantically, but when Carol arrived beside her, the swing was empty. The girl was gone.

"Wait, where did she go?" Kate scanned the garden, her panic rising.

Mrs. Peterson looked at Kate, her face full of concern. "She walked out that gate after you took off," she said, as though everything were perfectly normal. "Are you okay, dear? You look pale."

Carol turned to Kate, squeezing her hands. "Who was it?"

"The girl from my nightmares!" Kate's voice was strained. "Same dress, same hair. On the swing!"

Carol gave her a worried look. "Do you want to go look for her?"

Kate paused, thought for a moment, then shook her head. "No. No, I'll be fine. Wow, that really freaked me out. Weird, right?"

"Okay, well, I have to get back to Bob. He'll try to leave early if I don't keep an eye on him." Carol patted Kate's shoulder, a comforting gesture, and walked back down the hall.

Kate turned and walked toward the last door in the hallway. Mrs. Peterson was already entering the treatment room. Kate glanced back out the window one last time. The flowers the girl had been holding were now scattered on the ground. She wasn't crazy. Mrs. Peterson had seen the girl too.

Three

The new new girl

Catherine shuffled down the hallway toward Mary's office. The aged wooden floor creaked under her hefty frame. She stopped at the closed door, reached out with her pudgy hand, and paused. She had already been here twice today. She was pushing it with Mary—under a lot of pressure as it was. The last couple of repairs to the orphanage had drained most of this year's budget, and there was still a long list of problems that hadn't been fixed. Every day brought a new challenge just to keep the building standing. Catherine hated when Mary got upset with her. It wasn't that Catherine couldn't do her job; she just wanted to make sure she was making the right decisions.

She hesitated but then knocked.

From the other side, Mary called for her to enter. Catherine twisted the chipped-glass knob and opened the weathered door, her nerves on edge. Mary's soft sigh from behind the desk told her all she needed to know. She'd made the wrong decision. Three visits was the limit, after all.

She began to close the door but froze when Mary spoke again.

"It's okay, Catherine. Come in, close the door."

Mary didn't look up from her paperwork, nor did she try to hide her irritation. Catherine slowly closed the door behind her and let her eyes adjust to the dim light. In contrast to the rest of the orphanage, Mary's office felt almost like a cave. The only natural light came from two slits in the dark red drapes, casting narrow beams of light onto the floor. One small lamp on the desk offered the only artificial light, and the ceiling fixture had only one bulb. The dark chocolate paneling and trim absorbed whatever light there was.

Catherine's eyes finally adjusted. She started walking toward the center of the room. Ages ago, before construction had begun, this room had been a dining room for a single family. Now, with the wing connecting the house next door, the orphanage could accommodate sixty-five children—seventy-two currently were living here. Catherine ran her hand across the antique credenza, stalling, unwilling to meet Mary's eyes just yet.

When she reached the two green high-back chairs in front of Mary's desk, she paused, resting a hand on each. The chairs had been in the library when the house was still a home. The desk, the bookshelves against the wall, and the freestanding globe in the corner were all hand-me-downs from the same library, now repurposed as part of the kitchen.

"I don't know what to do with the new one," Catherine began, her voice tight. She rubbed her hands nervously on the back of the chairs.

Mary didn't respond immediately. She finished jotting down a few lines on her budget sheet, the silence stretching between them. Catherine leaned forward on her toes, rocking back onto her heels, her anxiety mounting.

"It's the new girl!" Catherine blurted out.

Mary put down her pencil and looked up slowly, her expression a mixture of patience and curiosity. "What about her? They said she'd be trouble. She's only been here an hour. I was hoping they were exaggerating."

Mary clasped her hands together on the desk and leaned back in her chair. "And what trouble has she brought?" she prompted.

"No, not the new new girl. John is with her in the activity room," Catherine said, her voice dropping low. "It's Larissa. She's the problem."

Mary raised an eyebrow. "What do you mean, Catherine?"

Catherine could barely keep herself behind the chairs as she spoke. "She hasn't spoken to anyone yet."

Mary didn't respond right away. She folded her arms across her chest and waited.

"It's only been a week, Catherine. Give her time," she said after a beat.

Catherine walked forward between the two chairs, placing her hands on the desk, and lowered her voice even further. "But then there's… the other thing."

"The other thing?" Mary's tone was patient but sharp now. The mystery of this new girl seemed to be drawing her in.

"She knows what I want her to do before I even ask. She does it with the other Sisters, too, not just me!" Catherine's hands clenched so tight against the desk that her knuckles turned white.

Mary's eyes softened as she leaned forward. There was a familiar tenderness in her voice as she responded, "Really, Catherine? This poor little girl is frightened. She's lost her father, has no relatives, and ends up here with strangers. She's probably trying to make a good impression by doing what she thinks you want done."

Catherine shook her head, still not convinced. Mary had seen that motion before—Catherine's fearful nod, a precursor to another meeting, another round of reassurance. Sometimes Mary wondered if she was here for the kids or for Catherine's anxiety.

"Okay, Catherine. Have her come and see me. I'll talk to her."

Catherine's face lit up, her relief almost palpable. "Thank you, thank you so much!" She started to back away, the blood finally returning to her fingers as she released the desk and clutched her hands together in gratitude. Behind her, the door creaked as it slowly opened.

The light from the hall spilled into the room, and Mary saw the silhouette of a young girl standing in the doorway.

"You wanted to see me," the girl's voice was a soft, clear whisper. It wasn't a question. It was a statement, calm and collected.

Mary's blood rushed to her neck, flushing her cheeks. She felt like she had been caught doing something wrong. Catherine let out a small squeak, dropping back into the armchair on the right.

"Yes. Larissa, dear, I did—uh, I do—come in." Mary stood quickly and motioned toward the empty chair next to Catherine. As Larissa entered, Catherine scurried across the opposite arm of her chair, putting more distance between herself and the girl.

Larissa sat down without a word, folding her hands neatly in her lap. She glanced at Catherine and smiled—a small, fleeting smile that seemed to touch only the corners of her lips. Catherine managed a brief smile in return, but quickly turned back toward Mary.

"If you don't need me, I'll go check on the new girl, Milda," Catherine said, her voice still shaky.

Mary absently nodded, "Sounds good, Catherine. Thanks."

Catherine didn't wait for another word. She rushed for the door, opening it swiftly and disappearing through it with a soft whoosh. The door slammed shut, the light withdrew, leaving Mary alone with the girl.

Mary frowned and absently spoke to the empty room, "I meant to ask her to bring me my glasses from the reading room. I left them in there during the meeting this morning."

As Mary settled back into her chair, her eyes drifted to Larissa. The girl's hair was full and wild, and she was still wearing the same white linen dress in which she had arrived. It was the one she wore whenever she could. Mary's lips curved into a small smile, but before she could speak, Larissa reached out and gently placed Mary's glasses in the center of the desk.

Mary froze. Her breath caught in her throat as she stumbled across the desk to retrieve the glasses. Her hand was only inches from Larissa's, but she could not quite look away from the girl's eyes. There was a depth there—gray-blue eyes that held something beyond their years. A sadness, wisdom, and an understanding that made Mary's chest tighten.

Larissa said nothing. She only stared back at her, calm and silent.

For a moment, Mary was unsure of what to do. She had seen many children over the years, but there was something about Larissa that left her speechless. She wanted to hold her, comfort her, protect her—but something in those eyes made her hesitate.

Compassion won out, as it always did with Mary. She moved around the desk slowly, never breaking eye contact with the girl. When she finally reached Larissa, she opened her arms.

Larissa stood, pausing for a moment in front of Catherine.

"Thank you," she whispered, her voice cracking. Relief, acceptance, and understanding seemed to fill the room. Larissa's smile grew a little, and for the first time, Mary saw something in her eyes—a glimmer of hope.

"You are very welcome," Mary said, pulling the girl into a hug. "And welcome to our home."

Larissa collapsed into Mary's arms, sobbing for the life she had lost and for what little she had left. Mary held her, weeping too. For this child, this small tragedy that had arrived at her doorstep.

As Mary wept, she whispered to herself, "The first has arrived. It has begun."

Four

GYM

Kate set the dumbbell back in its place and grabbed her towel, trying to shake off the weight of the week. The extra gym sessions Carol had suggested had helped, but the unease from her recurring dreams still lingered. The dream itself had grown darker, and now that Kate had seen the girl at work, it felt like everything was leading somewhere—she just didn't know where.

Carol, ever the optimist, had made it her mission to distract Kate from the unsettling feelings. The gym had become their refuge, the steady hum of elliptical machines and the soft clinks of dumbbells offering a familiar comfort.

"You're sure you don't want to grab a smoothie after this?" Carol's voice broke through the background music, a playful lilt in her tone. "You've got the rest of the night to just… forget about everything."

Kate glanced around the gym, taking in the usual scene. A few familiar faces, some older members who'd been there as long as the equipment, a couple of college kids showing off more than actually lifting. The air smelled faintly of sweat and rubber, but there was a calming rhythm in it all. She didn't need distractions; she needed to clear her mind.

"Honestly, Carol, I'm not avoiding anyone," Kate said, offering a half-smile.

"I just want to focus on my workout. That is all."

Carol raised an eyebrow, her gaze sweeping the room. "Focus, huh? So, what, you are not in the mood for 'the usual'?" She gestured around the gym. "It's Thursday night, a quick workout followed by a smoothie, maybe some light conversation, and the occasional flirtation."

Kate took a deep breath, shaking her head slightly. "I'm serious. I just want to clear my head. I've had enough distractions lately."

Carol's face softened, a knowing look passing between them. "Fair enough," she said with a sympathetic smile. "But if you're off to punch something, I'll be heading to the showers. You're on your own for that one."

"Thanks for the support," Kate replied with a grin. Carol's way of offering comfort was just the right mix of lightheartedness and reality.

Kate made her way over to the boxing area, weaving between the weightlifters. Putting a pair of gloves on, She took a moment to assess the first bag, then lined herself up just like she'd seen in the movies: feet apart, fists raised. She pulled back her arm and threw a punch with all the strength she could muster.

The bag swung forward a bit too aggressive and collided with a man who had been walking too close.

"OW!" he yelped, stumbling backward.

Kate winced and clutched her throbbing hand to her chest.

"What the hell?" The man stood up, more surprised than angry. He looked to be in his thirties, with a jump rope tangled around his feet, the result of not noticing the bag in motion.

"shit, sorry," Kate said quickly, trying to defuse the situation, taking her glove off as her hand throbbed painfully.

Not looking up the man continued, "Why would you hit the bag without checking….?" His tone was sharp at first, but when he finally looked up and met her gaze, it softened. "If there was someone on the other side…"

Kate softened too. Her hand was sore, but now she felt more concerned about his fall. "It's my fault," she said, bending down to pick up the mat he had dropped. "I wasn't paying attention."

"No, no," he said, shaking his head. "I was walking too close to the bag. My fault." He extended his hand. "I'm Dillan."

"Kate," she replied, shaking his hand. His grip was firm, genuine. It surprised her, and for a moment, she forgot about the pain in her hand.

Dillan looked at her hand, concern flashing in his eyes. "How is your hand? Can you move it?"

Before Kate could respond, he gently took her hand, inspecting her fingers and wrist with careful attention. She felt her face heat up at the sudden warmth of his touch.

"Ouch," she muttered, wincing as he lightly pressed on a tender spot.

"Sorry, sorry," he said quickly, letting go. "You'll definitely have a bruise, but nothing seems broken."

Kate rubbed her hand absentmindedly, feeling slightly awkward at the sudden intimacy. Dillan took the mat from Kate, and repositioned his gym back over his shoulder, as if ready to leave, but then stopped, looking back at her.

Kate raised an eyebrow. She half-expected him to walk away again, but to her surprise, he seemed to be gathering his courage.

Finally, he blurted, "Hey, you want to grab a bite to eat tomorrow night? Maybe catch a movie?"

Kate blinked, caught off guard by the suddenness of the invitation. Her mouth opened slightly, and Dillan quickly added, "I mean, uh—if you're free?"

The room seemed to hold its breath as Kate tried to process it. Dillan's nervousness was endearing. She couldn't help but smile, her nerves easing a little.

"I'd love to," she said, then, with a teasing edge, added, "How about Giovanni's? And can we do Saturday?"

"Yeah, that sounds great," Dillan replied, grinning like he'd just won a small victory.

"Seven o'clock okay?"

"Yeah! Seven's perfect." Dillan was practically glowing now, a smile so wide it was contagious.

"Okay, I'll meet you there," Kate said, slinging her towel over her shoulder. As much as she was looking forward to the punching bag, she felt the need to exit the scene. But she couldn't deny the buzz of excitement running through her, giving a little bounce as she took of the other glove. An real date. She couldn't remember the last time she'd felt like this.

Dillan practically skipped away, his previous nervous energy replaced by an eager rush. Kate watched him go, a smile tugging at her lips. Maybe this was the distraction she needed after all.

She turned toward the locker room, still smiling. Carol would be furious, she missed this.

Five

Two of them

As Catherine flew down the stairs to the first floor, she could not help but worry that Mary would again see this as an annoyance. It hadn't even been an hour since their last discussion. But this was too important to worry about upsetting Mary.

"Mary!" Catherine came running down the hall, her voice a mix of panic, heavy breathing, and urgency. Mary hearing her calling for her, could not help but to automatically be filled with irritation. It hand only been a hot minute since the last issue with the new girl, what could possibly be the problem now? Mary braced herself for another long day.

Catherine hit the office door hard, throwing it open, but holding her position.

"Mary! Come quick, the world is ending!"

"What?" Mary's face started to heat up.

"The activity room—come on!" Catherine was already halfway down the hall, not waiting for a response.

Mary followed quickly, her mind racing. The activity room was where all the children would be at this time of day. As she ran, she grabbed her rosary out of habit, murmuring a quick prayer under her breath.

They reached the stairs that led to the second floor, the only stairs in the building. Mary caught up to Catherine on the stairs, passing her as she hurried up them. By the time they reached the activity room, Mary could hear the chaos through the door. The room was a mess, an utter disaster. Books and papers flew around like confetti, and the noise was deafening, a hum like a generator in the background.

Neither Mary nor Catherine moved to open the door right away. They just stood, frozen, staring through the glass. The ceiling was raining office supplies, and there wasn't an inch of the room untouched. The sight made Mary's stomach churn.

"Holy—" Catherine jumped as the crack of an exploding desk sent shards of wood flying toward the window.

Mary quickly turned the handle and rushed in. Her eyes scanned the room, taking in the sight of Sarah and Agatha, two of the teachers, huddled with the children in the corner, trying to shield them from the chaos.

The paper and debris was everywhere. The low hum filling the air came from nowhere and everywhere. The floor felt like it was coming apart beneath them.

"It's the new child!" Catherine screamed, her voice barely audible over the noise. But Mary could hardly hear her. She was trying to make sense of the situation, trying to account for everyone's safety.

John appeared at Mary's side, his voice clear above the chaos. "Her name's Milda!" He pointed toward the center of the room. "That's her!"

Through the whirlwind of flying papers and furniture, Mary saw her, a little girl, maybe six or seven years old. Her hair was standing on end, her eyes wide and wild. She was at the center of the storm. As she passed a chair, it lifted off the ground, exploded into pieces, and crashed back down in a pile. The room was rapidly filling with trash, more than anyone could clean up in a day.

Mary couldn't help but think about the mess—the cleanup would take forever. But right now, the priority was getting everyone to safety. She stepped forward, but John's hand shot out to stop her.

"It's no good. As soon as you get close, she starts breaking more things.

It's not safe."

Mary hesitated. "We must do something. How is she doing this?"

John shook his head. "I don't know. All I know is… she didn't want to share."

Mary's frustration built. "What do we do?"

Someone else had joined them by the door as they were assessing the situation. Larissa had lined up with them assessing the chaos. Without a second thought, she started walking toward Milda, as though she were headed to meet a friend.

"Wait!" Mary called, but Larissa was already too far away. As they rushed to stop her, pieces of furniture came flying toward them, forcing them to leap out of the way. John helped Mary to her feet as Catherine, comfortably curled up in the fetal position, stayed safely out of harm's way.

Within seconds she was standing next to Milda, as calm as if she had just stepped into a quiet room. Milda looked up at her, wide-eyed.

Larissa smiled down at her, placing her hand on Milda's shoulder. Milda's hair started to settle back into place, and the room began to calm. Papers slowly floated to the ground. The heavy pieces of furniture crashed into the floor, and the loud hum faded.

"This is quite a mess," Larissa said, looking around at the debris. "Come on, it's lunch time. They're serving macaroni and cheese."

Milda's face lit up. "I love macaroni and cheese!"

Larissa smiled. "I know."

As the two girls walked toward the door, the last few papers floating down seemed to part around them like a slow-moving current. John and Mary stood frozen in place, their jaws slack.

Milda stopped just short of the door, turning back toward the children huddled in the corner. "Wait!" she called, then hurried over to the group.

She reached down, offering a blue crayon to a boy named Sam. "Here ya go," Milda said casually. "I'm done with the blue one."

There was a beat of silence. Everyone just stared at her.

With a soft sigh, Milda placed the crayon on the floor in front of Sam, then turned and skipped back to Larissa.

"Morning, Mrs. Mary," she called out as she passed.

Mary could only watch, wide-eyed, as the two children exited the room. Catherine, gave up the fetal position to move out of Milda's path crawling awkwardly over broken furniture, with pieces of crumbled paper and splintered wood sticking to her robe.

The door closed behind them, and the last of the confetti-like papers floated to the ground.

A book fell off a shelf. The lights flickered once more.

Mary stood there, overwhelmed. The second one had arrived.

One thing was certain—she was not prepared for the third.

Six

Lunch gossip

C arol wasn't one to bother with the crosswalk. She was a "live on the edge" kind of girl, and today, she was in a hurry. She sprinted across the street, earning three honks and a hand gesture before she reached the median. She paused, looking back at Kate, who was still making her way across the road at a much slower pace.

"Hey! Come on! You're walking slow on purpose!" Carol yelled.

"I'm not! I just want to arrive alive!" Kate gestured at the traffic.

Kate hadn't told Carol about Dillan the night before—mostly because it would have led to an endless search for the guy on every social media site. But by Friday morning, she couldn't keep it in any longer. She had a date. She'd kept every juicy detail about her encounter with Dillan a secret until lunch. Carol, not pleased with having to wait "an eternity," had picked the closest restaurant. She needed to know, and she was determined to do that as soon as possible.

Nick's Deli was nothing more than a small window and a green door on the sidewalk. Inside, the space was cramped and mismatched—tables and chairs haphazardly scattered through a narrow room. Along one wall were deli cases, and at the counter stood a small register. Nick and his family ran a simple operation: sandwiches, chips, and two soups of the day.

Kate and Carol walked to the back of the deli where the line started, debating over what to order. After some back and forth, Kate settled on a cup of minestrone and half a ham and Swiss on rye, while Carol opted for a cup of broccoli soup and a turkey and provolone sandwich on wheat. Carol had insisted on an early lunch, so at 11:00, Nick's was practically empty. The Friday crowd always arrived later.

They chose the one table in front of the window. Carol slid into her seat, leaning forward with her hands clasped together like she was about to pray. Kate, on the other hand, calmly sat down, adjusting her napkin, opening her sandwich, and setting her soup just right. She tried to hide her smirk as Carol began fidgeting, clearly itching to hear the story.

"Okay! Spill!" Carol demanded, nearly bouncing in her seat.

"Okay!" Kate finally let go, leaning forward, unable to contain her excitement. "So after you left me and I headed for the punching bag."

"You mean I was still there, and I missed him?!"

"Yeah, if it wasn't for you, I probably wouldn't have gone to the punching bags, so shh."

"Okay, sorry, go on. Punching bags…"

"Right, so I walked over, reared back, and punched the bag as hard as I could. And then I practically broke my hand."

"Oh my God, what happened?!" Carol's eyes were wide with concern.

"I thought I had really hurt it at first. It was throbbing, and I couldn't move it. But after a minute, it started feeling better, and I could wiggle my fingers."

"Enough about your hand! When did Dillan come in?"

"Okay, so I guess he was standing on the other side of the bag, and when I hit it, I knocked him over. He was pissed, of course. And I was pissed too, because my hand hurt."

Carol waved off her comment. "Yeah, heard about the hand, but back to the boy."

"Geez, okay! So we were both mad, but then we saw each other, and suddenly we were all nice."

"Nice!"

"Yeah, nice. So he's all concerned about my hand and starts checking it out, like really checking each bone in each finger."

"Oh my God! He's a doctor!" Carol sat up; eyes sparkling.

"That's exactly what I thought!"

"Or a surgeon!"

"I know! Or a specialist or something, but he's definitely in the medical field!"

"That's awesome! You are so lucky! All I ever meet are mailmen and store clerks." Carol grinned as she glanced around the deli.

Kate shifted in her seat, catching sight of the busboy out of the corner of her eye.

"Sir, can we get some more water?" she asked.

The busboy moved over to their table, pouring water into their glasses. "Kate? Is that you? Hey!"

Kate blinked and turned her attention to him, her face faltering for a second before she quickly recovered.

"Dillan?" she asked, her voice dropping slightly.

Carol's eyes widened, and she turned to face Kate, clearly confused. Dillan had just gone from "Dillan the Doctor" to "Dillan the Dishwasher."

"Carol, this is Dillan." Kate introduced him with a bit of awkwardness.

Kate felt for a split second, something unspoken passing between Carol and Dillan. It wasn't much, but it felt loaded. Almost like they recognized each other, and maybe… knew each other.

But then, just as quickly, the moment evaporated. Carol smiled at the busboy like she had no idea who he was. "It's nice to meet you," Carol said, shaking her hand before quickly turning her attention back to Kate.

"So, you work here?" Kate asked, still trying to recover from the shock of it all.

"Yeah, I've been working here for about two weeks," Dillan replied, leaning slightly closer to Kate. "It's a good gig for me."

"Oh, are you going to school?" Kate asked, though she was still processing the change.

"No, I just need time off on short notice sometimes, and the boss is pretty understanding."

"Oh," Kate replied, turning back to Carol. "Carol and I work across the street at the rehab center."

"Wow, what do you do?" Dillan asked, still fixed on Kate.

"We're physical therapists."

"Wow, that's awesome. Must have been a lot of school for that."

"I guess."

"Well, I better get back to filling water glasses," Dillan said. "I'll see you tomorrow night! Really looking forward to it!"

"Uh, yeah. Me too," Kate said, her voice slightly strained as Dillan walked away.

Both women stared at each other for a moment, stunned. Carol finally broke the silence.

"He seemed… nice," she said, her voice flat.

"I knew it! So he's a busboy and not a doctor." Carol turned back to watch Dillan walk away.

"I'm sure you'll make very beautiful babies together, who will grow up to aspire to take crappy jobs just so they can take time off whenever they want." Carol ribbed.

Kate looked defeated.

Carol reached over and took her hand. "I'm just kidding, I'm sure he's a great guy. You probably don't have the full story yet. Wait until after the date, then make your judgment on his career choices."

Carol sat back in her chair and giggled, and Kate couldn't help but join in. She could never stay upset with Carol for long.

"You're right," Kate said, glancing over at Dillan, who was bent over, picking up a customer's napkin that had fallen under a table.

"And he has a really cute butt," Kate added with a grin.

The two women giggled and teased each other as they finished their lunch. Their gossip session turning into an amusing memory.

Seven

Just for the weekend

"Have you ever seen anything like that?" Mary hadn't said a word as she and John made their way to her office. But once the door was closed, she couldn't hold it any longer. The words rushed out of her in hysterics. "I don't think I am ready for this."

"We've seen some amazing things over the years," John said calmly, though his exterior was for Mary's benefit. Inside, he was spinning, his mind racing.

"But nothing like *that*!" Mary's hands waved in agitation. "Chairs flying around. Exploding!"

John watched her pace. He was doing the same thing in his mind, trying to process what they had witnessed. He waited until he felt he could keep his cool before speaking.

"That was incredible. Who was the other child? Where did she come from?"

"That was Larissa. She arrived about a week ago. She's different too," Mary said, still pacing.

"She's different too?" John raised an eyebrow.

"Yes. I think she can see the future. She knows what's going to happen."

"Did you see how the new girl calmed down and everything stopped flying around when Larissa touched her?"

"Yes! What is going on here?"

"God works in mysterious ways."

"Through children and exploding furniture? Can't we get a simpler sign?"

"If it were simple, what would be the point? We need to think this through and decide what to do."

"I know one thing—this new girl can't stay here. The other kids are afraid of her. Hell, I'm afraid of her!"

"Mary, you need to calm down. Get a hold of yourself. She's just a little girl."

Mary stopped pacing and turned to face him. The disbelief in her eyes was palpable, but she didn't need words to express it.

"Yes, you're right," John said slowly. "This is more than just a little girl. How about I take her home for the weekend? We can figure it out after that."

John watched her pace again, the idea clearly settling in her mind.

"Last time you said that you ended up adopting Kate. What was that—fifteen years ago?" Mary let out a little chuckle. "You said you'd take her home for the weekend and never brought her back!"

John shook his head, a hint of a smile playing at the corners of his mouth.

"What can I say? I like charity cases." Kate had been John's world since the first day he'd met her. She had won him over the first time she looked up at him with her sad blue eyes.

"Well, this little girl is different than Kate. John, I think she may be dangerous."

"So she can make chairs fly and explode in mid-air. She needs guidance, not fear. That doesn't make her dangerous."

Mary stopped pacing again, this time locking eyes with him. "Are you prepared for the kind of guidance a girl like this will need?"

"Well, that's something we'll have to figure out. Besides, I have Kate. She can relate to what this new girl is going through." John was confident Kate would be able to help, though he wasn't sure how she'd feel about it.

"Okay, John. Let's give it a try. Maybe the other kids will forget about the incident by Monday." Mary chuckled again lightly, but the memory of what they'd witnessed would stay with her.

John stood up and headed for the stairs, his mind still swirling with questions. He reached the second floor, took a left at the landing, and walked toward the third door on the right—his familiar path. It seemed like just yesterday he'd made this trip to talk to a little girl who was struggling. That was 15 years ago, and she'd become his daughter. Now, here he was again, heading for the same door.

"Am I ready for this?" he muttered under his breath, though he knew the answer already. He wasn't sure, but he would walk through that door. He would do whatever it took to fix the problem.

John stopped at the door, hand on the handle, and took a breath. "You aren't ready for this," he said to himself. He turned the handle and stepped into the room.

It looked the same, maybe a little paler than he remembered—perhaps the paint had faded. The wooden floor was worn in the middle from years of little feet heading off to bed, night after night. The orphanage had always been short on funds, and freshly painted walls and varnished floors were luxuries they couldn't afford. John walked forward, the boards beneath his feet squeaking. He smiled. He remembered that squeak.

The room had twelve beds, six on each side, old and creaky. Ten dressers lined the walls, one between each bed. The middle beds were always assigned to the younger girls. On the left side, near the middle dresser, Larissa and Milda were opening drawers, packing.

"Wow, you two really made an impression on the teachers," John said as he sat down on the bed opposite the open suitcase. Both girls paused for a moment, glanced at him, then turned back to their packing without a word.

"Where are you going?" John asked. "Are you planning on running away?"

"Nope," Larissa replied, handing clothes to Milda to put in the suitcase.

"No? Well, then why are you packing?"

"We're getting ready," Milda answered without looking up.

"Getting ready for what?"

"To go home," Larissa said, matter-of-factually.

"Ah, well, where is home?"

"Don't know."

"If you don't know where home is, then why are you packing? How will you find it?"

"You're going to drive us," Larissa said, like it was the most obvious thing in the world.

John blinked, trying to process. "Okay, well, let's stop playing games. Why don't you come home with me for the weekend? I have an older daughter who's always wanted a baby sister—or two. You can get away from the crowds here and see how it goes."

Milda paused her packing and looked at John like he was slow to catch on. With a long sigh, she explained, "That's why we're packing. To go home with you."

"Oh, well, I hadn't asked yet. How did you know?"

"Sissy told me."

"Sissy?" John raised an eyebrow.

Larissa raised her hand, gesturing to Milda. "Sissy," she confirmed.

John blinked in confusion. "Did Mary let you know I was coming?"

"Nope. I saw you coming," Larissa said with a grin.

"You saw me coming up the stairs?"

Larissa beamed. "Yep."

John's mind raced. *She saw me coming?* It dawned on him that Larissa had some ability to know the future, but it wasn't clear how much she understood herself. Milda, ever the practical one, let out another loud sigh, this time with more impatience.

"Ugh, nooo. She can see things that happen in the future! She told me you were coming to take us home and that we'd meet Kate tonight!" Milda finished closing the suitcase with a snap and began pulling it off the bed. Larissa helped her, and the two girls moved toward the door.

John was still processing, sitting as still as a rock, his mind struggling to catch up. He finally shook his head and stood up, trying to gather his thoughts.

"Okay! Well, then let's get a move on!" he said with forced enthusiasm.

Larissa and Milda turned to each other. Larissa smiled knowingly, while Milda just shook her head in disbelief.

Eight

Together at last

Carol had decided on a Friday night shopping trip for Kate's date with Dillan the "Dishwasher". According to Carol, Kate needed an outfit that would make a boy want to stand up, get a real job, and become a man. Kate could always count on Carol to move on quickly and not keep ribbing her.

Kate's phone went off on the entry table, the special ring she had for dad, Carol gave Kate a smirk as they both lunged for the phone. Carol, the clear winner, answered it and gave Kate a sultry look.

"Hi, Dad." She was dripping inappropriate vibes, grinning from ear to ear. It was gross having a best friend who still had a crush on your old man.

"Give me that!", Kate shoved her keys into her mouth and lunged at Carol with both hands. After a couple of minutes of playful keep-away, Carol reluctantly handed over the phone.

"Hwhehy DwawD!" Kate took the keys out of her mouth and tried again.

"Hey, Dad!" She rolled her eyes. "Yeah, that was Carol," Kate held her palm over the phone and whispered at her. "Dad says hi." She stuck her tongue out, and Carol laid her chin on her shoulder, blinking rapidly back.

On the other end of the phone, Kate's dad cleared his throat. Never a good sign. The last time he'd done that; it was to tell her that her goldfish had died. John got to the point quickly.

"I'm bringing some girls home with me, and I'd like you to stick around and meet them."

Kate wasn't prepared for this. "You're what?"

"A couple of the girls had a bad day at the orphanage, and I'm bringing them home for the weekend to give them some breathing room."

"Dad, do you think this is a great idea? You're not as young as you once were," Kate said, the only excuse she could come up with, and it sounded lame even to her.

"I'd really like for you to hang out and meet them. They could use a friendly face."

"Okay, I'll wait here. Yep, love you too." She hung up and tossed the phone into her purse.

Carol jumped in front of her, dying to hear the other end of the story. "What the heck was that about?"

"Dad's bringing home two girls from the orphanage."

"Oh, did you tell him you were out of milk? He can pick that up too while he's grabbing a couple of kids!"

"I guess they're causing trouble, and Mary asked if he would take them for the weekend." Kate stared blankly at herself in the front hall mirror.

"Don't you always tell me you were just supposed to come home for the weekend?"

"Yeah…" Kate's voice trailed off.

"Hmm." Carol stopped staring at Kate and hip-checked her out of the mirror, then pulled out her lipstick. "Pucker up."

Kate shrugged off her sweater and draped it over her purse. "This is different, though. There are two of them, and there's no way he thinks he can handle two kids now."

Carol froze in front of the mirror, holding her "I'm not just a waitress" red lipstick to her bottom lip. She glanced back at Kate through the reflection. "Yeah, at his age, what is he—40?"

Kate shot up from staring at the floor and met Carol's glance in the mirror.

"He's 50!"

"Ah, dang. He looks good for 50!" Carol mocked sizing him up, hands on her hips.

"Carol! That's my dad. It creeps me out when you go all, *oh, your dad is soooo cute!*"

"Sorry, just call them how I see them." Carol shrugged.

"Anyway, he's about 10 minutes away. He wants me to hang out and meet the girls." Kate knew her dad had a soft spot for troubled kids and had watched him over the years reach out to any child he thought he could help. She had to admit, though, that she had been waiting for this moment.

She picked up her sweater and hung it in the front hall closet. "You'll have to go out without me tonight."

"Oh no you don't! This is going to be way more fun than trying on clothes!"

It was finally starting to sink in, even before meeting the two new kids. They'd be staying for more than just the weekend. It was how her father was. He would open his house—and his life—to kids who needed help. He had done it before, but only one had stayed permanently.

Kate remembered coming home for the first time like it was yesterday. All the other kids thought she was weird, and she'd had trouble making friends at the orphanage. She hadn't thought about it much lately, it felt like such a long time ago.

She remembered how it felt to walk in the front door. How scared she had been. John had laid out hot chocolate and cookies. They sat at the dining room table silently for what seemed like hours, sipping and nibbling. She finally felt at home here with John, she'd never forgotten that first night. Kate decided this was a memory she would pass on to the two girls on their first night at home. As she got to work, it finally dawned on her why she loved hot chocolate so much. The smell of safety, in a cup.

By the time Kate heard the keys jingling in the front door, she had the drinks made and laid out on the kitchen table. She was just finishing putting cookies on a tray—because what's hot chocolate without a cookie or two? As she rounded the kitchen, heading for the dining room with the tray, the two girls appeared in the front doorway.

"Holy shit!" The cookies fell off the tray and scattered across the vinyl floor. Both girls gasped, and John quickly shut the door behind them. All four of them froze for a moment—Kate staring at Larissa and Milda and back again. Carol sat at the table, watching cookies roll in every direction.

Finally, the cookies stopped wobbling. Milda leaned down, picked one up, and took a bite.

"Nice to meet you, Kate." Milda grinned through a mouthful of crumbs.

"Holy shit!" Kate gestured wildly between the girls and John, waiting for him to explain.

"Uh, you said that already." John dropped the bags and began picking up the cookies.

"Holy shit!" Kate slapped her hand over her mouth and slumped into the nearest chair.

Milda turned to Larissa. "You know, I thought she'd be a little more refined. Hey! Hot chocolate!" Milda pulled out a chair for herself, picking up a cookie from the cushion and putting it on the plate in front of her.

"Dad! These are the girls from my dream!" Kate said, wide-eyed.

John paused, then placed a couple more cookies on the table. "The way today's going, that doesn't surprise me."

The rest of the evening passed in a strange kind of fog.

After the shock wore off somewhat, Kate managed to keep her hands from shaking long enough to take a sip of hot chocolate. She stared over the rim of her mug at Larissa and Milda, who were sitting side by side, acting as if this was just a regular Tuesday night and not the moment her entire reality cracked wide open.

"So," Kate said slowly, setting her mug down. "Want to explain how you crawled out of my nightmare and into my kitchen?"

"That's wild," Milda whispered. "I've never been in someone's dream before. Was I the cool one?"

"You were the loud one," Kate deadpanned.

"Yeah, that tracks."

Carol, who had been mostly silent, gave a soft snort. "Sounds about right.

She could talk her way through a coma."

"Thank you," Milda said brightly, as if it were a compliment.

Larissa looked uneasy, like she'd been caught in someone else's bad dream on accident. "We were hoping you'd explain that to us."

Kate paused, then took a deep breath. "I should probably just tell you everything. The dream. All of it."

And so she did.

She told them about the dream—how it always began in a massive warehouse, cavernous and cold, with shelves and crates splintered like matchsticks. Everything was broken, as if a storm had torn through the place. Dust hung thick in the air, turning every breath into a struggle. To one side, the entire roof had collapsed, forming a jagged mountain of rubble and twisted metal beams. The flickering overhead lights cast eerie, stuttering shadows across the shattered floor, making the destruction seem alive and shifting. Somewhere behind her, Kate could always sense others—people moving or watching—but no matter how hard she tried, she could never see their faces. And in the center of it all: Larissa, lying motionless on the floor, and Milda, screaming for help—her voice raw and panicked, echoing off the warehouse walls like something from a nightmare Kate couldn't wake from.

Then the dream always shifted—never abruptly, but with a heavy sense of dread that settled deeper into Kate's bones. She would find herself on her knees beside Larissa's lifeless body, the concrete cold and gritty beneath her. Milda was on the other side, her eyes wild with desperation. Without warning, Milda would grab Kate's hands, forcing them onto Larissa's chest. Her small fingers dug into Kate's wrists as she cried out, "Help her! Please, help her!" over and over again. Kate would try to pull back, shaken, frightened, but Milda wouldn't let her. "I can't," Kate would say, helplessly—again and again, the words like broken glass in her throat.

But eventually, Milda would stop. Her grip would loosen. Her hands would fall away, and Kate would yank hers back instinctively, as if burned. Then Milda would slump forward, her head and arms dropping onto Larissa's chest, her sobs dissolving into a quiet, aching mantra: "Help her… help her…" The lights would continue to flicker, dust would swirl in the silence, and that's when Kate would always wake up—gasping, heart racing, the sound of Milda's voice still echoing in her ears.

A silence fell over the room. The kind that hummed with too much held breath and too many unsaid thoughts. No one moved. The only sound was the soft ticking of the kitchen clock and the distant hum of the refrigerator. Kate stared at her hands in her lap, still feeling the phantom weight of Larissa's body beneath them.

Then, quietly, Milda said, "Well… that's dark."

She glanced sideways at Larissa, who was pale and wide-eyed, staring at the floor like she'd seen the scene herself.

"I—I didn't know it was that bad," Larissa said finally, her voice tight. "That I—" She stopped herself, shaking her head.

"You're not dead," Carol added quickly, trying to be light but not quite pulling it off. "You're sitting right there. Breathing. Annoying me. So… definitely alive."

"I'm sorry," Kate said suddenly, looking between them. "I didn't want to tell you. I thought it was just a dream. Just… something weird. But then you showed up—*you*—and it was the same faces from that warehouse, and I—" She cut herself off, overwhelmed again.

Carol shifted in her seat, arms crossed. "Okay, so, that's a lot. I mean, not your run-of-the-mill stress dream. I usually just dream I forgot to study for a test."

"It wasn't a dream," Milda said, this time serious. "Or… not just a dream. You saw something. Something real."

Kate looked at her. "You think it's a vision?"

"You saw something that hasn't happened yet." Larissa's tone was low.

Milda scratching at her neck. "But why did Kate see it and not Larissa?"

"Because she's one of us," Carol muttered, almost to herself.

That earned her a sharp look from Kate. "One of what?"

Carol didn't answer. She stood and grabbed another cookie from the tray, her expression unreadable. "I need a drink of water," she said, disappearing into the kitchen.

Milda sighed and leaned back in her chair, twisting her necklace around her fingers. "I'm not saying it's definitely going to happen… but if it *does*, maybe now we can stop it."

Larissa nodded slowly. "Yeah. Maybe that's why you saw it, Kate. So, you could change it." Lying, knowing that was not how visions worked.

Kate stared into her hot chocolate, watching the marshmallows slowly melt away. "I just hope it never happens."

John eventually convinced everyone to get some rest, though none of them seemed eager to leave the kitchen. The night ended with sleeping bags spread across the living room and whispered questions bouncing between couch cushions until the soft weight of exhaustion settled over them all.

Nine

Date night

By morning, the energy in the house had shifted. Larissa helped John make pancakes, Milda spent twenty minutes deciding between four outfits she now called "her apocalypse looks," and Kate… Kate mostly wandered around in a state of emotional whiplash.

Every time she looked at the girls, she felt that creeping sense of déjà vu—the kind that came with knowing fate had already placed them on a path none of them fully understood.

The only positive thing was there was no nightmare last night, she figured it was because now she was in the nightmare.

That afternoon, John had left to look at some new windows and doors for the orphanage, promising to be back in time for Kate's date.

Milda and Larissa were at the table trying to glue a wooden plant holder back together that Milda had somehow knocked over with her backpack. Kate and Carol found themselves alone in the kitchen.

"I still can't believe they're real," Kate muttered, staring into her coffee cup.

Carol leaned on the counter beside her. "You'll get used to it. Eventually."

Kate looked sideways at her. "You think you can get use to Milda?"

Carol raised an eyebrow. "Define used to."

A loud thump from the living room followed by Milda shouting "I said I was sorry!" made both girls smile, briefly.

"You think I'm crazy?" Kate asked softly.

"I think you're living in a world that got turned upside down," Carol replied. "And I think you're handling it better than most would."

Kate took a breath, nodded. "Yeah. I guess."

The weight lifted a little.

Later that evening, Kate stood in front of her bedroom mirror, nervously twisting a strand of hair while Carol fussed behind her with a curling iron like a stylist on a mission. Larissa sat cross-legged at the foot of the bed, offering quiet but thoughtful fashion commentary, while Milda sprawled across the pillows dramatically, balancing a throw pillow on her head.

"I'm just saying," Milda declared, "if he doesn't gasp the moment he sees you, I say we dump soda in his gas tank."

"Please don't," Kate muttered, adjusting her sweater for the fifth time.

"I'm kidding! Mostly... Maybe just slash one tire," Milda grinned, then flopped onto her stomach and added in a mock-serious tone, "You know, this is basically the red-carpet moment of your suburban teenage life."

Carol raised an eyebrow as she pinned the last curl in place. "Ignore her. You look great. Way less haunted than you did this morning." She twisted her head to look over her shoulder at Milda, "And where in the world did you even hear that, you're like a 30-year-old trapped in a six-year-old body"

"Seven!" Milda said sharply, throwing the pillow to the ground, rising to her feet, jumping feverishly on Kate's bed. "But you do look very pretty."

Kate rolled her eyes, but a smile tugged at the corner of her lips. For a moment, things felt almost normal.

Her phone started to ring on the edge of the dresser. Kate glanced at the caller ID, flashing "Dad" and then the time—half an hour past when he was supposed to be home—she already knew she wasn't going to like what he had to say.

"I'm sorry, Kate, really I am, but I'm still in Newark."

"But, Dad, I have a date tonight." Kate could already feel the frustration building. "I can't babysit these two." She glanced at Larissa and Milda, both turning their full attention towards the drama unfolding. Milda plopped down next to Larissa on the edge of the bed, started eating pretend popcorn, and sharing it with Larissa, who of course took a big hand full of popcorn air.

"I'm sure he'll understand," her dad continued. "Just call him and let him know. Change it to tomorrow night."

"I don't have his number. We were just supposed to meet," Kate said, walking into the kitchen, trying to get a little privacy.

"Well, take them with you. Explain the situation and set another date. I'm really sorry, honey."

"Fine! You owe me!" Kate hit the done button and dropped the phone on the counter harder than she intended, letting out a sharp breath.

"Sweet! We get to go on a date!" Milda had followed her out and was leaning half hidden on the kitchen wall.

"You're not going on a date," Kate said, grabbing a muffin from the kitchen island, breaking off a hunk and shoving it in her mouth. "I am just going to ask Dillan if we can move the date to tomorrow night." She stuffed the rest of the muffin in. While she was distracted, Milda shot a quick glance at Larissa, who had wandered out with Carol bringing up the rear. Larissa put a finger to her lips. Milda locked her lips and pretended to throw away the key.

Kate caught the look out of the corner of her eye. "Oh, no. I don't care what you think or what you think you saw," she said, waving her hands between the three of them. "You are not going on my date with me."

Giovanni's was in the heart of the old downtown district. Kate had picked it more for the atmosphere, although the food was good. The brick-paved sidewalks and fancy streetlamps made for perfect after-dinner strolling, especially when paired with the pretty shops and coffee spots nearby—perfect for a first date. Well, except for the two kids in tow.

Kate parked as quickly as she could and got out. Larissa and Milda were already on the sidewalk, waiting for her.

"Wow, you guys aren't wasting any time, huh?" Kate laughed as Milda grabbed her hand and pulled her toward the entrance.

"Is he cute?" Milda tugged on Kate's hand, desperate for the answer.

"Yes, he's very cute." Kate scanned the parking lot, searching for Dillan.

As they reached the front door, Kate leaned down so the girls could hear her. "Okay, here's the deal. You're going to say nothing. You're just going to stand there and smile. Got it?"

"Not a problem, sis," Larissa said, catching the door and walking through. "For me…"

Kate paused, glancing at Larissa. "What exactly do you mean?"

Then it dawned on her. "Milda!" But it was too late. In the moment Kate turned her attention to Larissa, Milda had already run up to Dillan and was holding his hand.

"Kate! Is this Dillan? He's really, cute!"

Kate's mind raced—should she just leave? Grab Milda and run out the door? It was just the first date, they didn't even know each other yet, they didn't even exchange phone numbers. She could just add this to the ever-growing list of bad dates. But how would she get Milda off him without starting an awkward conversation? No way around, she was going to have to face him.

Kate walked toward Dillan, reaching out for Milda. "I'm so sorry. My dad had to go out of town, and we're watching some kids this weekend. I didn't have your number, or I would have called. Maybe we can do this another night?" She pulled Milda into her, quickly cupping her hand over Milda's mouth before the girl could say anything else.

Dillan smiled and handed a menu to Milda. "No worries. We can just get a table for four." He turned to speak with the hostess.

Milda, wide-eyed, opened the menu and read aloud, "What is es-car-got?"

Larissa leaned over her shoulder to see. "It's snails."

"Eww! That's the grossest thing ever!" Milda wrinkled her nose and stuck out her tongue. Then she turned to Kate and said louder than necessary, "Who would ever want to eat a snail?"

"Shh!" Kate hissed, trying to keep her voice down while flashing a nervous smile at the other diners who were clearly staring at them.

Milda continued, ignoring her, "Honestly, why would anyone even try one? They're slimy and dirty!"

The maître d'—who had been standing near Dillan—turned his head with a look of disgust before facing Dillan again. "I'm sorry, but we have no tables available."

Milda, undeterred, stepped closer to Dillan. "That's okay. They don't even have macaroni and cheese here. You wouldn't want to eat in a restaurant that doesn't serve macaroni and cheese. This place is crazy!"

She cupped her hands around her mouth and shouted, "What are you people doing? They serve snails!"

The maître d' spun around, wide-eyed, darting his gaze between Dillan and Kate, clearly hoping they'd do something. Dillan, laughing so hard that he had tears in his eyes, managed to say, "Well, what do you expect? You don't even serve macaroni and cheese!" A few people at nearby tables chuckled.

Kate, horrified, stepped forward, cupping her hand over Milda's mouth again, and started backing toward the exit. "I'm so sorry. We'll be going now."

As she tugged Milda along, Dillan followed, wiping his eyes, still laughing.

Kate mouthed at Dillan "I am so sorry." Dillan nodded it off, still trying to catch his breath.

Milda wriggled free of Kate's grip as they reached the door. "Exactly! What kind of place is this?"

Once outside, Kate spun Milda around, her eyes wide and teeth clenched. "What is wrong with you?"

Milda took a step back, fear flickering in her eyes. "Nothing! What's wrong with all those people in there?"

"For the rest of the night, I want nothing to come out of your mouth," Kate said, mimicking zipping her lips and tucking the key into her pocket.

Kate sighed, brushing her hair back from her face. "So… maybe we can try this another night?"

Milda made a disapproving sound and shook her head. Dillan, ever the good sport, placed a hand on Milda's shoulder. "Nonsense. We're already out, so why don't we find a good restaurant? One that serves macaroni and cheese?"

Milda's eyes lit up. "Yesss! Mac and cheese!"

Kate looked at him for a minute, then smiled. "Alright, if you're still up for it, I'm starving." They all turned and started walking down the cobblestone street.

Milda grabbed Kate and Dillan's hands, tugging them along. "There's this great pizza place up ahead! You get to make your own pizza!"

Kate, dragging her feet, groaned. "I really don't feel like going to Crazy Pizza tonight. It's always packed and noisy. I'd rather eat somewhere else."

Larissa caught up on the left side of Kate, grabbing her other hand. "You may not feel like it, but that's where we're going."

Kate sighed dramatically. "Fine. Crazy Pizza it is."

Milda jumped up and down, pulling Dillan with her. "Yeah! Crazy Pizza! Dillan, aren't you excited?"

Dillan, playing along, grinned. "I'm so excited, I can't even contain it!" Milda giggled, then stopped mid-skip. She tugged Dillan down to her level. "Dillan, how do you feel about dogs?"

Kate, shaking her head, muttered, "Please, no."

Dillan, smiling at the question, responded, "I love dogs. In fact, I often pretend I am one. Arf, arf!" He barked enthusiastically.

Kate facepalmed. Larissa laughed. Milda burst into giggles. "I knew I was going to like you!"

By the time they had reached the front of Crazy Pizza, they'd managed to scare two couples into crossing to the other side of the street. But, two young boys had joined the barking festivities, so it wasn't a total loss.

Milda was first through the door and immediately insisted on a booth near the cooking area so she could watch her "masterpiece" cook.

Crazy Pizza was a family-friendly, themed restaurant. The mascot—a large, goofy duck with wild eyes and a purple-orange sports jersey—was plastered on everything from the menus to the walls. Booths lined the walls, and tables of various sizes filled the middle. To the left, a door led into the game room, and past that, the bathrooms. The layout was designed to ensure the kids stayed busy and talked their parents into a few extra bucks for games. At the far end of the restaurant were stations where kids could make their own pizzas. Parents loved it because it gave them at least fifteen minutes of uninterrupted adult conversation—though with blaring music and a squawking duck, most just ended up staring at each other in silence.

Once they settled into the booth and ordered drinks, Milda bolted toward the pizza-making station. Larissa excused herself, promising to keep Milda out of trouble. Dillan chuckled and handed Larissa a ten for the game room.

Larissa started to walk away but turned back. Dillan had his back to her, and Kate was watching her go. Larissa winked and gave her a thumbs-up. Kate sighed, muttering under her breath about Dad, timing, and how fate had it out for her. Dillan turned around in his seat to see what she was talking about. Larissa darted away, giggling.

"What did I miss?" Dillan asked, looking at Kate.

"Nothing," she replied, shaking her head. "Absolutely nothing."

"Your sisters are great. Milda knows exactly what she wants, huh?"

Kate froze. "They're not my sisters—well, I mean, I think they are? Never mind," she said, picking up a menu to hide her confusion.

Dillan raised an eyebrow. "Okay… well, whatever they are, they're great!"

He leaned back, turning his head and throwing his arm over the back of the booth to get a better look at Milda and Larissa at the pizza stations. Milda was tossing a miniature pizza dough in the air and catching it—until she got a little too enthusiastic and the dough flew across the counter, landing in a vat of sauce. Sauce splattered up onto one of the employees helping the kids. Milda and Larissa both quickly looked away, pretending to focus on their pizzas. With no dough left, Milda poured sauce onto her plate—making an even bigger mess. The worker took the plate, swapped it for a fresh one, and placed a new blob of dough in front of Milda. Larissa turned to shrug at Kate and Dillan.

Milda started to mash out her dough, ready to try the toss again. Dillan burst out laughing. Kate just shook her head, eyes closed in exasperation.

"Yeah, they're great," she said dryly. "I've had more chaos in the last two days than I have in my entire life."

The waiter arrived, dropping off a Caesar salad for Dillan and a house salad for Kate, with ranch dressing on the side. Kate immediately flicked the onions she'd asked to be removed onto a napkin, then began mixing the dressing. She took a few bites, still talking between chews.

"It's just that I started having these dreams, and then the girls from my dream *showed up* in my life! What the heck is that? And my dad is just being all, 'Oh well,'" she air-quoted the last part with her fork, accidentally flinging a bit of ranch dressing across the table. "I mean, really—this is the craziest thing ever!"

Kate finally glanced over at Dillan, who was staring at her with wide eyes. Realizing she'd been spitting food as she talked, her face turned bright red. She quickly covered her mouth with one hand, grabbed a napkin with the other, and began cleaning up the mess.

"I'm so sorry," she muttered. "I'm not usually like this. Ever since they showed up, I've just... I've been all over the place."

Dillan wiped a piece of lettuce that had nearly landed in his lap. "No, no, it's alright. So, you had a dream about them?"

Kate nodded, still embarrassed. "Yeah, it really freaked me out." She took a breath, steadying herself.

Dillan, sensing her discomfort, reached across the table and gently slid his hand over hers. His touch was warm and steady, a quiet kind of reassurance. She looked up, startled by the gesture at first, but when her eyes met his, something inside her settled. Without thinking, she turned her hand palm-up and curled her fingers between his. They were holding hands—just like that—and the room felt a little less heavy.

"Before you met them?" Dillan asked softly, his thumb brushing once across her knuckles.

"Yeah. The dream was so vivid. The girls were the same." Kate put her fork down, suddenly wary of any more food mishaps.

Dillan turned his head to look at the girls again. Milda was getting another fresh plate of dough from a different pizza worker, who also had sauce splattered across her uniform.

Kate leaned forward. "What? What's going through your mind?"

Dillan turned back to face her. "I don't know, Kate… but I doubt what you had was just a dream."

Kate frowned. "What do you mean?"

"If you were dreaming of those two specific girls *before* you met them, I'd call that a vision."

Kate's stomach dropped.

"What is it?" Dillan reached out instinctively and grabbed her hand.

"In the dream… Larissa's dying," Kate whispered, pulling her hand back and folding both of her hands in her lap.

Dillan moved forward but then paused, retracting his hand. "I'm so sorry. I'm sure I'm wrong. It was probably just a dream." He sounded more upset than Kate expected him to.

"Let's not talk about it anymore," Kate said quickly, pulling her salad plate toward her and stabbing at it with her fork.

"Yeah, you're right. Let's talk about something else." Dillan agreed, mirroring her gesture and eating quietly.

They finished their salads in silence. When the girls joined them, they distracted themselves with talk of Milda's future as a pizza chef and other random topics, mostly revolving around Milda's antics. At the end of the night Dillan walked them to the car, there wasn't much left to say. They just listened to Larissa and Milda's endless chatter as they headed back up the cobblestone street.

At the car, Larissa and Milda said their goodbyes to Dillan and climbed in the back. Dillan opened the driver's side door, resting his hand on the top of the door.

"I'm really sorry I even suggested that" Dillan said.

Kate on instinct, reached up and placed her hand on his, both of them surprised at the touch. "I know, me too," Kate replied with a heavy sigh. "It's just… it's a lot to handle—having them in the house, and then all this other stuff…"

"Good night, Kate," Dillan nodded.

"I had a really nice time," Kate Said.

"So did I." Dillan smiled, his eyes softening.

On impulse, Kate leaned in and kissed him gently on the cheek. "Be careful driving home."

He nodded, a bit stunned, opening the door wider, her cheeks flushed as she passed by him and slid into the driver's seat.

Dillan shut the door behind her leaning down to wave at the girls in the back. Both returned a big grin.

Larissa raised an eyebrow as Kate looked into the rearview mirror to check her path. "So... we're kissing now?"

"Shut up," Kate muttered, trying not to smile.

"About time," Milda added from the back.

As they pulled away, Kate let herself smile fully, her fingers still tingling from the touch of Dillan's hand.

For the first time in a long time, hope felt real.

"Way to go, Dillan." he muttered under his breath. As soon as Kate's car was out of sight, Dillan pulled out his phone

"Jack, yeah, it's me, yep, I met all three of them. I think we have a problem though. I will come by in a bit". Dillan hung up his phone, let out a heavy sigh and kicked a bit of trash in the street before heading to his car.

Ten

Sandwich shop confrontation

It had been almost a week since Larissa and Milda found themselves swept into Kate's world—one of visions, secrets. In that time, they'd been adjusting to living with Kate and her dad, John. For all the chaos surrounding them, it was starting to feel weirdly… normal.

That morning, the three girls had gone shopping. Milda desperately needed clothes that weren't sleep shirts borrowed from Kate, and Larissa had finally admitted she couldn't keep wearing the same white linen dress without someone saying something about "vintage style" at school.

After hitting two stores and nearly losing Milda in a dressing room mirror maze, they stopped at Kate's new favorite deli—*Nick's Deli.* The girls had ribbed Kate every time they had stopped here. Clearly it wasn't Nick's famous Pastrami on Rye that Kate couldn't get enough of.

Inside, Dillan worked the counter like always—smirking just enough to be charming and slicing meats with unnerving precision. He gave Kate a wave and disappeared into the back, probably to prep their usual.

Kate had gone inside to grab their order, leaving Larissa and Milda in the car, which was parked just around the side near the alley where deliveries were dropped off.

Larissa was scrolling idly on her phone when Milda suddenly sat up straighter.

Milda nudged Larissa and pointed, "Hey… check out that cat on the dumpster"

Larissa glanced slightly and went back to her phone.

"I'm bored." Milda dropped back down on the seat, folding her arms. As she watched the cat pacing on the edge of the dumpster. Two hooded figures walked up, the shorter of them reaching up to pet the cat. Both of them stood silently watching the side exit to the deli.

"Well this looks promising." Milda sat up and threw her arms around the head rest in front of her. The side door to the alley opened and Dillan walked out. The two figures lowered their hoods and immediately started a heated discussion with Dillan.

"Hey, Isn't that Dillan in the ally?

Larissa looked up. Sure enough, Dillan was standing on the sidewalk at the deli's delivery door, in what could only be described as a low-key but intense argument with two people.

One was tall, lean, and he had tightly coiled energy like someone used to barking orders. The other looked broader, hair tied back in a short ponytail, arms crossed, she was unreadable. They were both dressed in mostly black, not enough to look suspicious—but just enough to not fit in.

Larissa leaned forward for a closer look, "That's… weird."

"They look like backup dancers for a villain." Milda pressing her face to the window.

The three spoke in low, fast tones. Dillan gestured toward the street, then back toward the deli. His jaw clenched. The tall one shook his head, said something sharp. The other shook her head, and started to walk away, towards where the girls were parked.

Dillan called out "KRIS! You know I am right! Jack, tell her."

The cat hissed at Dillan and dropped from the dumpster to the ground.

Kris stopped and turned around, responding to Dillan in a tone too low for the girls to here.

All three of them just stood there for a moment.

Finally, Dillan stepped back. Said one last thing and walked briskly back into the deli, brushing his apron down and vanishing through the back door.

Jack jogged to catch up to Kris the cat right behind him. They all started back toward the girls.

Larissa and Milda ducked in their seats as the two strangers past in front of the car. They didn't look in, didn't glance their way. Just kept walking, mid-conversation.

"Jack, I know Dillan's right, but it isn't that simple." Kris said looking around like someone was following them.

"I think it is, either she gives up or we take her down" Jack responded.

The words floated through the slightly cracked window like a spark falling on dry leaves.

Larissa and Milda froze.

Milda sat back up, feeling the danger had passed, "Take who down?!"

"I don't know… but that was definitely not about sandwiches."

The strangers turned the corner and disappeared.

The girls sat up, starring back at them through the front windshield was the cat.

"Holy Shit!" Milda exclaimed pushing back in the seat. The cat looked from Milda to Larissa and back again. Then turned, twitched her tale and trotted off around the corner.

Larissa took a deep breath. "What they hell was that?"

Milda turned towards Larissa, true concern, "Do we tell Kate?"

"If we do, she'll freak out. And she *likes* Dillan. She might think we're just being paranoid."

"Well, I *am* paranoid. And that was still super weird. And that cat was freaky"

They both sat back as the deli door jingled, Kate emerging with three sandwiches and a cookie bag she clearly wasn't planning to share. A huge smile on her face gave the girls the answer to their question.

Kate opened the door and threw the sandwiches on the front seat

"Okay, I got the pastrami monsters. Hope you two didn't eat the seats while I was gone."

Kate shifted into the seat and started the car. "Oh, Dillan insisted on me bringing cookies for both of you too" Kate took a cookie out of the bag for her and threw the bag into the back seat. Milda grabbed the bag, drew out the biggest cookie and started devouring it. Larissa, leaned back in the seat, the cookie bag in her lap.

Larissa and Milda exchanged a glance. Nothing was said. Larissa pondered, Milda munched, but both knew something had just shifted.

Eleven

Tea party

❦

Kate woke the next morning to the sounds of light jazz coming from her alarm clock. She walked down the hallway, following her normal routine, heading to the kitchen to make coffee. One eye half opened she maneuvered through the dining room where she could make out the two girls sitting at the table playing quietly. She continued her way thankful things were calm at this time of morning. She opened the cabinet and pulled the coffee down from the shelf as the doorbell rang.

Larissa looked up from the table, "I wouldn't get that!" she exclaimed. Kate was already heading for the door.

"Why would I not answer the door?" Kate peaked through the peep hole. Mr. Peterson, from 310 was staring back at her. Kate lifted the chain and unbolted the lock.

"Mr. Peterson?"

"Hi there Kate, I hate to bother you, but Ginny is missing." Mr. Peterson was trying to peek around Kate hoping to catch a glimpse of his Ginny.

"Ginny?" Kate tried to open her other eye, but without that first cup of coffee it was rather difficult.

"Ginny. My dog Ginny? She's a black and white Papillon." Mr. Peterson motioned his hands about six inches apart to show how big.

"Oh, your dog! No, we haven't seen any dog" Kate started to close the door. As a high-pitched yelp came from down the hallway.

"What was that then?" Mr. Peterson started across the threshold.

"Yeah? What was that?" Kate turned and eyed the girls; both eyes were now fully open.

"You don't want to know." Larissa turned around and concentrated on the dining room table activities. Kate started towards the hallway when a small black and white dog ran around the corner and jumped into Mr. Peterson's arms.

"Ginny! I thought you hadn't seen her?" Mr. Peterson was not happy.

"We hadn't, I hadn't, I, I, I just got up." Kate was back pedaling but she wasn't sure why.

"You know everyone told me the tenants in this building were so nice and trustworthy, I haven't been here but three weeks and already you are trying to steal my dog?" Mr. Peterson turned and walked quickly down the hall cuddling and baby talking to his Ginny.

"I didn't know she was in here! Honest!" Kate was hanging out the door yelling down an empty hallway. She closed the door, bolted the locks and turned her attention to the dining room which was suspiciously quiet.

"You stole the neighbor's dog?" Kate had her hands on her hips and her head cocked to the side.

Milda threw her hands up in the air, "We didn't steal it! It just showed up at the door." She belted and stood up on the chair throwing her hand on her hips, mocking Kate.

"So, what, you let it in to play tea party with you?" Kate motioned at the table that was all laid out, continuing her rant.

"Hey! What are you guys doing with Grandma Anne's China? That China is really old; it came over on a boat from England with Grandma Anne! We only use that when old people come to visit!" Kate was walking around the table lifting cups and moving plates closer to the center so that they wouldn't get knocked off.

"Wait! My clothes! Who said you could wear my clothes? And hats and necklaces and shoes! Not my shoes! Dad!" Kate stared off towards the bedrooms.

Milda turned on the chair to face Kate who had started towards the hallway.

"WE! are having a Tea Party. You can't have a tea party without a tea pot and cups and saucers." Milda started moving the items back to their proper position around the table. Larissa picked up an empty plate and motioned it to Kate.

"Do you have any sugar cubes?"

"Uh…No. DAD!" Kate was pacing back and forth between the table and the hallway not sure whether she should go and get her father or stay and watch over Grandma Anne's delicate China.

Larissa motioned the plate in Milda's direction, and in her finest British accent, "Milda would you please?"

"Certainly" Milda sat back down in her chair facing the kitchen.

The apartment was the typical three-bedroom open floor plan, there was no real definition of where a room ended and one began with the exception of the bedrooms and the bathrooms. From the dining room table where the two children sat and Kate was standing, hands on her hips in the perfect pose of indignation, you could easily see the entire well-maintained kitchen.

The lid to the sugar jar unscrewed and dropped gently to the counter. A miniature sugar tornado began to flow out of the jar and into the air. It swirled around for a few seconds and then started to flow towards the dining room table where it collected in a granulated pool just above their heads. Water from Larissa's glass rose up and joined the sugar. As the sugar and water mixture floated down towards the table it began to separate into smaller areas, so that by the time it reached the empty plate in the middle of the table there were several perfectly formed sugar cubes.

"Thank you Dear Milda!, Lovely, now we can have our Tea Party" Larissa pulled her napkin off her plate and placed it in her lap with an overly flourished flick of her wrist exactly like she had seen in those old English movies of people having afternoon tea.

"No Worries, lady Larissa" Milda mimicked Larissa's napkin fan fair, adding an English accent with a pompous attitude. Obviously, Milda had seen those old English movies as well.

"What the hell was that?" Kate removed her hands from her waist and repositioned them a little higher for emphasis.

"One lump or two?" Larissa grabbed the tongs and started for the newly formed sugar cubes.

"Two Please" Milda held her teacup out by the saucer, in the proper English manner.

"What the hell was that?" Again, Kate repositioned her hands a little higher which did nothing but get her a little closer to doing the chicken dance.

"It's sugar, would you like one lump or two?" Larissa was putting the last cube into Milda's cup and was maneuvering the tongs for another cube.

"I know it is sugar; how did you get it into cubes?" Kate was officially ready for the chicken dance. Milda turned to face Kate and mimicked her chicken dance hand stance "Didn't you see it float through the air? Do you need glasses?" Milda put the last piece of her biscuit in her mouth and concentrated on her tea.

"Yes, I saw it! No, I don't need glasses! How did that happen?" Kate was not giving up.

"This is a lovely tea party! May I have another biscuit?" Milda returned her attention to the tea party and motioned to the table in general.

"Why certainly, here you are dear." Larissa gently placed another biscuit on Milda's plate and snickered at the state of Kate's hysterics.

"DAD!"

"What? What is going on?" John finally came out from his bedroom still in his PJ pants and a V-neck undershirt.

"Crazy stuff is going on! These two are going to have to go!" Giving up on the chicken dance, Kate started waving her arms around at the children, the table and the kitchen as if this would let him know what he had missed.

"Hey, a tea party! May I join you?" John started for one of the empty chairs at the table.

"Sure, we would love to have you!" Larissa made a polite bow from her sitting position and motioned to the seat in between Milda and herself. John pulled the chair out and sat down

"Dad?" exasperated. Kate went back to her chicken dance stance.

"What? Hey, when did we get sugar cubes?" John took the fine linen napkin off his plate and placed it gently in his lap, mimicking the two little girls' English playtime.

"One lump or two?" Larissa offered the sugar plate, pinky out for effect.

"Two please." John held out his cup, pinky out of course.

Kate stormed out of the room mumbling about the crazy people surrounding her

"What is wrong with her?" Milda thumb pointed towards the hallway where Kate could still be heard marching to her bedroom.

"Stress, she needs to relax, she should have joined our tea party." Larissa placed the sugar cube plate down and started on her biscuit.

"I'll go talk to her. Please excuse me" John pushed out and laid his napkin across the chair.

John reached Kate's door and knocked lightly.

Kate, can I come in?

I don't know, are you going to make something fly, or perhaps bring home another person from my dream?" John had opened the door and was standing just inside the threshold.

"Dad, this is wigging me out!" Kate was in her bed, covers pulled up around her.

"It's freaking me out too kiddo" John moved to sit at the end of the bed. He reached out and rested his hand on her right leg. Kate pulled the covers off of her head and turned to face her dad.

"What is going on? This isn't just you trying to help another troubled kid."

"No, this is definitely a whole new ball game" John started rubbing Kate's foot, this was more for him to relax then her. The truth was this was wigging him out too. Kate sat up in bed.

"Dad, really what is this all about?" John fidgeted for a minute and then turned back towards Kate. She was an adult now; she could handle the truth. Although John wasn't entirely sure he could handle this truth.

"Ouch!" Milda Screamed.

"Mr. John, come quick" Larissa was screaming from the dining room.

"Milda broke a cup from the China set and cut her finger!" Larissa was at the end of the hall when John came running out of Kate's bedroom. Kate was right behind him. John scooped up Milda and immediately applied pressure to the finger. It was a bad cut. There was already quite a bit of blood. By the time Kate handed John a linen from the table, his hand was dripping blood onto the floor as well. John wrapped Milda's hand tight in the napkin.

"Milda are you okay?" John set Milda back down on the chair.

"I am fine, Sorry about the cup" Milda motioned to the floor where bits of China laid.

"Don't worry about the cup, we can always get another cup. Kate come put pressure on this" John couldn't tell if the cut was already soaking through the napkin or if all the blood on the outside of the napkin was from his hands. As Kate took to applying pressure, John quickly moved to the kitchen to wash up. Kate grabbed another napkin from the table and switched it out for the blood soaked one.

Kate peaked at the cut, "Dad, this is too deep, we are going to need to take her to the ER and get stitches" Kate covered it again and applied pressure but already the napkin was turning red again. John had been thinking the same thing. "I'll run go get the car." John grabbed the keys and ran out the door.

Kate scooped up Milda still holding her hand around Milda's finger.

Milda threw her good arm around Kate's neck and leaned into Kate's chest. "I am really sorry about the cup" Milda's eyes were welling up.

Kate smiled down at Milda, "Like Dad said, it's just a cup, we can get another", "Larissa, get my purse on the counter?"

Larissa grabbed the purse, ran to the front door and held it open for Kate to go through. "Larissa, can you lock the door?" Larissa already had Kate's keys out and was turning the bolt.

Milda brought her head up "It is feeling much better now!"

Larissa threw the key back in the purse and turned to Kate, "She will be okay now"

Kate had already started down the stairs, "She will be after we get some stitches in her finger"

Milda started to unwrap her finger, "It really feels okay now, I don't think we need to go to the hospital"

Kate was already getting out of breath, freaking out and carrying a kid down a flight of stairs was better exercise then the elliptical.

"It may feel better now, but we still need to make sure we get stitches in it so that it heals correctly."

Milda was fidgeting more and trying to pull her finger back out of Kate's grip.

"I am better now; can we finish the tea party now?"

By the time they got to the front door of the building they could hear the car screech to a halt. Larissa opened the lobby door, Kate flew through sideways like a professional. John already had the back door open waiting with a panicked look on his face.

Kate got in the back seat still holding Milda and John shut the door.

"Larissa let's get you in the other side"

John and Larissa ran around to the other side of the car and Larissa settled in and buckled. John jumped in slammed the car in drive and the tires screeched as John maneuvered into traffic while still buckling himself in.

"I don't' suppose either of you will believe that she is okay now?" Larissa was calmly sitting staring out the window at the traffic.

"I know she will be" Kate said rocking Milda back and forth.

"I am fine, can't we just go back to the tea party?" Milda was trying to climb out of Kate's lap into the seat next to her but Kate was not letting go of her.

"Dad, do you think she is in shock? Shouldn't she feel some kind of pain? Look at all this blood!"

"It's hurting now!" Milda starts to squirm in Kate's arms

"Okay that's good, I was worried you were in shock."

"No, you're holding it too tight you are hurting my fingers!"

Milda tries to wiggle her fingers out of the towel

"Stop, I have to keep pressure on it" Kate tightens her grip on the towel.

"LET GO!" Milda's face turns red and her hair starts flying around her head. The towel rips into shreds and falls through Kate's fingers.

"Oh my god! Dad were going to need another towel or rag or something, she just blew it up!" Kate was searching the back of the car trying to find something else to stop the bleeding

"Look at her hand" Larissa sat staring out the window ignoring Kate's hysterics.

Kate looked down at the hand and the bleeding had stopped, just the smallest bit of redness near where the huge gash had been.

"What the hell! Where did the gash go? There was so much blood!" Kate had had enough of this, this on top of all the other crazy stuff going on was too much for her.

"It's gone; I tried to tell you that she would be alright" Larissa looked over at Kate hoping that she would settle down.

"What you can heal yourself too! Sugar flying through the air, healing yourself! This is too much, Dad, you didn't mention anything about this. What the hell else can they do? Turn me into a toad?" Kate wasn't going to be settling down for the rest of the year at this rate.

"She didn't heal herself" Larissa returned to the window gazing; this conversation was going to take a while.

"So, you did this? Did you heal her?"

"No."

"So, who did this?"

"You did!" Larissa turned and faced her again.

"I did? How?"

"I don't know how we do anything; we just do?" Larissa exclaimed.

"I don't understand?"

"You healed her, you fixed her cut"

Milda grabbed Kate around the neck and hugged her "Thanks!" She chimed in.

"But I couldn't have", Kate returned the hug and then sat her down in the middle of the seat

"You think I am lying about it?"

"No."

"Then accept it, we are related"

"Related?"

"Similar, we all have powers"

Milda climbed back on Kate's lap facing towards her "Can we go back to our tea party now?"

Kate repositioned Milda on her other knee. "Related, like cousins or something?"

"Yes, something like that, I guess" Larissa said, knowing that Kate wouldn't believe the truth at this moment.

Milda placed her hands on each side of Kate's head. Turning her head so that she had her full attention. "'Can we get a dog?" Milda chimed.

John chuckled from the front seat, as he was finding a place to make a safe u-turn.

Kate turned her eyes to face Larissa, her head still firmly held between Milda's hands. "So you don't know really if we are related? Are you guessing or do you know, like you knew Milda's hand would be okay?" Kate was starting to settle down a little.

"I have never had a dog." Milda continued.

Larissa sighed; this was a conversation she had tried to have with her dad a long time ago. "It isn't like I have an almanac that I am reading, it comes and goes, usually when the situation is stressful"

Milda pivoted so that she could meet Kate's eyes, still holding her head. "Any dog would do; it does haven't to be a fancy dog"

"Well, I am very stressed! How about you spill some more information!" Kate squirmed to break free from Milda's grasp with no success.

Milda tightened her grip, "any stray dog will do, it doesn't have to be store bought"

"Would you stop with the dog already?" Kate grabbed Milda's hands and removed them from her face.

John tried to contain a giggle in the front seat.

Kate glared at him in the rear view mirror.

"Dad! You could help here! Pulling information from a 13-year-old is like tug a war with straws!"

John just couldn't hold it anymore and let out a belly laugh, "You are doing just fine love"

Kate glares at him and then turned her glare to Larissa, Larissa does a disgusted sigh and then blurts out

"We are sisters alright!"

"Sisters?" Kate dropped Milda's hands starring at Larissa. Taking advantage of her free hands Milda grabs Kate's head again, "Now can we have a dog, Sis?"

Kate's eyes go blank, and her face starts turning red, "Of course, sure, it makes perfect sense, two kids show up, all kinds of crazy things happen, and it turns out we are sisters, sure that explains everything"

Larissa turns back to the window

"I knew this was going to be difficult for you, I really didn't want to spring this on you like this"

Kate very slowly turns back to face Larissa, dragging Milda's hands with her.

"Difficult, why would it be difficult, I mean there is what 7 years difference between you and me and how old is Milda?"

"I'm 7! And I want a dog! Hey, my birthday is coming up! You could get me a dog!" Milda is bouncing up and down on her leg.

"You really expect me to believe we have the same mother and there is a 14 year difference between me and Milda?" Kate isn't having anything to do with the sister thing.

"Yes, I do, but I was pretty sure you wouldn't believe it if I told you like this, so now we will have to spend the next several hours going back and forth about whether or not we are really sisters, which is turning out to be fun! Not as much as getting my teeth cleaned but oh yeah this is fun!"

"December 11th, that's my Birthday, it's like two weeks away!" You could get me a dog for my birthday!" Milda continued to turn Kate's face back to her and bouncing even more.

Kate struggling once again to turn back to Larissa "Look this is a little hard to swallow, and this has been a crazy day! How about we just stop talking about it for now"

Kate leans her head back on the seat and closes her eyes Milda's hands still firmly planted on each side. Trying to make sense of the last day and this new information. She had always wanted sisters, but this is a little different then she had pictured it. Kate just couldn't wrap her head around the possibility that they could all be sisters.

Milda grabs the back of her neck and pulls her head back up so that they are eye to eye, nose to nose.

"You know two weeks is not a lot of time to pick out a dog, we should start right away, and December 11th is right around the corner!"

Milda let her neck go and Kate dropped her head down on the back of the seat again closing her eyes and mumbling, "Yeah that is all I need, a dog."

John parked the car in front of their building, turned around to face them, still trying to suppress the grin, still failing.

"I am so glad that you are enjoying this!" Kate pouts

"Why don't we go back up and I will make us some lunch?"

Milda excited about the idea of food, jumps off of Kate's lap and starts to open the car door.

"Yeah I am starved!"

John starts "How about…" Larissa interrupts "Macaroni and Cheese is fine" John continues "….Okay." John smirks at Kate, turns back around and shuts the car off.

Kate catches his eye in the rear-view mirror, "Tell me you can't see this is going to get really annoying?"

John laughs "Nah, I love it! Of course, I am going to have to watch what I think from now on though!"

Milda grabs John's hand as he is reaches the sidewalk, "Can we finish our Tea Party?" Milda blinks her little blue eyes at him and he smiles "Of course we can, after we clean up the mess"

Milda smiles and does a little jump and pumps her fist.

"Yes! I already cleaned up the mess!"

"You did, how?"

"While we were sitting here talking" and up the steps she runs.

John turned in amazement looking at Kate as he started towards the stairs. Milda stops halfway up the front steps and turns around, putting her hands up towards John. He scoops her up and she throws her arms around his neck.

Milda leans into his ear and whispers so that no one can hear.

"Can we have a dog?"

Kate who is just reaching the bottom of the stairs.

"No! We are not getting a dog! And we are not borrowing the neighbor's dog!"

Milda pulls back and stares John square in the eyes.

"How about I let you think about it?" Adding a wink for good measure.

"Okay, I will think about it." John said with a smile. Milda hugged him around the neck again as Kate started shaking her head and mumbling to herself about stinky dogs, irritating children, and the similarities between her dad and a spineless jellyfish.

Twelve

Finding out

John's alarm clock blared at 4:30 AM. He sprang out of bed with surprising energy, eager for the day ahead. He had a date with an old church scheduled to be demo'ed next Tuesday. John hoped to score some much-needed window hardware from the old building. The retired pastor had also mentioned a set of stained-glass doors that might just fit the gap between the dining hall and sitting room at the orphanage. He'd agreed to meet the pastor at 7:00 AM, and with the long drive ahead, he was already running late.

After tying his shoes, John quietly stepped into the hallway and closed his bedroom door behind him. A low rumble vibrated from the spare bedroom where Larissa and Milda were sharing a bed. He paused, listening carefully. The rumble continued, almost like a growl. Curiosity piqued, he crept closer to the door and cracked it open.

Inside, Larissa and Milda were fast asleep in the queen-sized bed. Between them, sprawled like a grey rug, lay a large dog—its tail on Larissa's pillow, its head at their feet. The beast let out a deep growl, louder now, until John opened the door wider. The dog immediately spotted him and, with a happy wag, sent Larissa's face into an accidental tail-whip. She batted it away, groggily swatting at the dog, while Milda reached over, still half-asleep, to pet it.

"Bob, go to sleep," Milda mumbled, her voice thick with sleep.

John chuckled under his breath, backing away from the door. "I'm going to pretend I didn't see that. Kate can deal with Bob and his owner," he muttered as he walked down the hallway, towards the kitchen. But as he turned the corner, he froze, startled to see Kate sitting at the dining room table.

She lifted her mug of hot chocolate, blowing on it. "Whose owner? And what am I dealing with?"

"Uh… the kids," John replied, hastily waving it off. "You'll have to deal with the kids. I'm running late." He kissed her on the head before heading for the door.

"Have a good day, Dad! Love you!" she called after him.

"Love you too," he responded, closing the door behind him.

Kate hadn't slept much the night before and had given up after her clock flipped 4 a.m. The lack of sleep was at least better than the nightmare, but she couldn't shake the unsettling thought that the two girls from her dream were now just down the hall. She tried not to think about it too much. Instead, she focused on what she'd do today.

Kate had decided sometime in the sleepless night to make a trip to the orphanage. Maybe speaking to Mary would provide some clarity. But with the girls in the house, she couldn't decide whether to leave them alone or take them with her. John would likely disapprove of her leaving them unattended but taking them along was another headache altogether. Maybe Carol could watch them for a bit?

Before Kate could decide if it was too early to call Carol, she heard shuffling feet in the hallway. It was barely five in the morning—didn't anyone sleep in? Larissa appeared at the corner; one eye barely open as she dragged herself toward the dining room. She grabbed the end of a chair and pulled it out with a quiet grunt.

"We're going with you today." she said, folding her arms and resting her head on the table.

Kate groaned inwardly. "Shit." She canceled the call and slumped back in her chair. Larissa chuckled.

"Larissa!" Milda's voice echoed from the bedroom.

"Great. Everyone's awake. Well, guess we might as well get started since we're all going," Kate muttered, heading down the hall to shower. Larissa, now wide awake, went to check on Milda. She opened the bedroom door, just a crack, then Bob came charging out, knocking her back into the hallway. Milda followed closely behind, and the trio rushed to the front door. Bob was scratching impatiently, desperate to get out.

"He's got to go. Real bad!" Milda said, her voice tinged with amusement. She threw open the door and Bob bolted outside.

"Well, you know Kate's going to lose it when she finds out about Bob," Larissa said, digging through the cupboard for a box of Pop-Tarts. She put one in front of Milda, who dug in eagerly.

"She freaks out about everything. She needs to chill," Milda mumbled between bites. Bob scratched at the door again, and Larissa let him back inside.

"She won't want us going with her once she finds Bob. I've already talked her into it, so this should be fun," Larissa said, winking.

"Did you tell her that you saw it?" Milda asked between mouthfuls.

"Yeah…" Larissa replied, though she wasn't entirely comfortable lying. But she had no other choice. Milda opened a second pack of Pop-Tarts, and the girls sat down at the table, planning their next move.

"We need to figure out how to sneak Bob into the car before Kate flips out," Larissa said.

"Why don't we let him wait down on the street? When we go to get in, he can sneak in and lie on the floor," Milda suggested, jumping up and opening the front door.

"Perfect," Larissa said. Milda tossed Bob the last of her Pop-Tart, and the dog trotted outside to wait.

The girls got ready quickly, but by the time they headed out, Kate was already standing by the open front door, keys in hand.

"Come on, you two! Let's get going!" she called.

Milda grinned as she rounded the corner. "Dang, you sound just like a nun!" she giggled, stepping past Kate and out the door. Larissa followed, grinning.

Downstairs, they climbed into the car, and the door was left ajar. Bob, ever the opportunist, peeked around the corner to ensure the coast was clear before leaping into the backseat with a soft thud. Milda slammed the door shut just as Kate glanced in the rear view mirror.

"What the heck is that?" Kate demanded, her jaw dropping at the sight of the massive dog occupying the backseat.

Milda scrambled to explain. "I can explain! I found him. We wanted a dog. And here he is!"

"That's not a dog; that's a prehistoric dinosaur!" Kate turned around to face her. "No way is that thing coming with us! There's probably a neighbor looking for their pet!"

"No, it's my dog," Milda insisted. "He came to me, honestly!"

Larissa tapped Kate on the shoulder. "It's true. It's her dog."

Kate turned, staring at Larissa in disbelief. "What do you mean, it's her dog?"

Larissa shrugged. "This dog will be with Milda for a long time, like it or not."

"Dammit!" Kate groaned, her patience hanging by a thread. "Why do I feel like I have no say in anything that's happening?"

Milda settled back into her seat, Bob resting his head on her lap. Milda leaned into the middle of the car, speaking in a low voice to Larissa.

"Did you really see me with Bob for a long time?" Milda asked.

"Sure did," Larissa replied, though a pang of guilt tugged at her. Lying didn't sit well with her, but it was necessary. Bob barked as if to back her up, and Larissa scratched behind his ears, wiping away the slobber.

The drive to the orphanage was quiet, each of them lost in their own thoughts. As they pulled up to the building, three faces looked out at the familiar structure, the place that held so many unanswered questions.

Kate paused at the front door, her hand hovering over the handle. Out of the corner of her eye she caught a glimpse of the same black bird from the courtyard at work. The same purple band around it's neck and red feathers. The bird bobbed its head back and forth as if motioning Kate to walk through the door.. As Kate didn't move, Milda pushed by seeing the bird on the window ledge.

"Hey, that is a cool looking bird!" Milda motioned to the bird, who squawked in her direction and then flew away. Kate came out of her trance and turned the handle to the door.

She had walked through this door countless times, but now it felt different—heavier. It seemed to hold the weight of her past and her future all at once. The girls filed inside, with Bob trotting in beside them, unwilling to wait in the car.

They headed down the hall toward Mary's office. The hallway was short, but it felt endless as Kate's heart raced in anticipation. Bob, however, had no hesitation. He was already scratching Mary's door.

"How does Bob know which way to go?" Kate asked, raising an eyebrow at Larissa.

"Psychic?" Larissa shrugged, clearly amused. "He's probably just smarter than the rest of us."

The door opened, and Mary stood there, as if she had been expecting them all along. "I've been told for years that you three would come to my door, but I never believed it would really happen," she said, stepping aside to let them in.

The room felt smaller with all of them here. Kate stood between the two chairs, The girls sat, Bob resting at Larissa's feet. As Mary settled into her chair, she reached for a simple wooden box on the shelf, pulling it down carefully. The box was unadorned, but Mary treated it as if it were made of the finest material.

"This box holds memories of the children who have come and gone through these walls," she said, opening it and carefully sorting through its contents. "Most of them are fond memories, like this cross made from Popsicle sticks. It belonged to a boy who was reunited with his father after he was presumed dead in an avalanche."

Mary placed the cross back and pulled out a photograph, handing it to Kate. Kate knelt between the two chairs so the girls could view the photo.

The picture was faded, the edges worn with time. There were two-woman, young adults, smiling for the camera. In the background, a Zeppelin loomed, magnificent yet foreboding.

"What's that big thing behind them?" Milda asked, her voice tinged with curiosity as she leaned closer to the photograph.

Mary shifted slightly in her chair. "That is called a Zeppelin, a type of blimp that was popular in Germany during the twenties. This one didn't get off the ground. Something went wrong, and it exploded, killing everyone on board."

Milda gasped, and Larissa instinctively reached out and put her hand on Milda's forearm. "So, did these two girls die?"

Kate stood up examining the photo more closely.

"Just one of them" Mary replied, her tone somber. "From what I know of the story, they both got on the blimp, but the girl on the right—her name was Eleanor—got off before it took off."

The room fell into a heavy silence. The girls sat, waiting for Mary to continue. Bob, ever curious, had settled his head back on Larissa's lap but shifted slightly so he could watch Mary intently.

"These girls were best friends," Mary said, her voice quiet, "but something happened between them. When they boarded the blimp, Eleanor locked her friend, Genevieve, in a room, then got off the blimp, leaving her behind."

Milda's eyebrows shot up in disbelief. "Well, that totally sucks! What kind of friend does that?"

Kate set the picture down on the desk, her brow furrowing. "Wait a minute... did Eleanor blow up the blimp?"

"Possibly," Mary replied, her gaze turning distant. "But it's more likely that she knew it was going to blow up." Her eyes lingered on Larissa for a moment. Milda's eyes darted between Mary and Larissa, a realization dawning on her.

"Oh! Like Larissa can see things... this lady could too?"

"That's what I think," Mary nodded. "I got this picture from a little girl named Gwen. She was about Larissa's age and had the same gift—the ability to see things. Gwen came to live here in 1984. She wasn't shy like Larissa, though. She was very talkative and would share her visions with the other children and the sisters. Word got out about her gift, and reporters came to interview her. They wrote a beautiful article, and we started getting more visitors."

Mary paused, her eyes momentarily drifting as she seemed lost in the past. "People wanted Gwen to predict the future. One day, she told me she knew the day she would leave the orphanage. I was excited, it's an amazing thing when a child gets adopted, it gives them a fresh start. But she didn't seem excited. She told me she'd miss the orphanage and all the friends she had made. I didn't think much of it at the time."

Kate could see where this was going. She leaned in slightly as Mary continued.

"One afternoon, we were all out in the courtyard. The other sisters and I were sitting on benches under the oak tree, and the kids were kicking a ball around. I noticed Gwen had wandered off to the far end of the field, away from the others. I called her, but she didn't respond. I decided to go check on her, thinking maybe she was having one of her visions and needed someone to talk to."

Mary's hands trembled slightly. "When I stood up, Gwen raised her hand, signaling for me to stop. I hesitated for a moment, then started walking toward her again. She raised both hands, pushing them out as if to stop me from coming any closer. I could see that she was crying, her face twisted with sorrow. Then, she smiled at me, and mouthed, 'Thank you.' Before I could process what was happening, there was a loud bang, and Gwen collapsed."

Mary stopped for a moment, wiping her eyes with a handkerchief. The room was silent. The girls could feel the weight of the story settling in around them.

"After that, it was chaos. Children were screaming, running around, but no one had seen Gwen fall. It felt like hours before I could move, but of course, it wasn't. I rushed over to her and knelt by her side. She had this picture in her hand," Mary said, gesturing toward the photograph on the desk. "She handed it to me, and I tried to help her, but Gwen stopped me. She told me she was going to die and needed me to listen carefully."

Mary's voice cracked, and the three girls leaned in, instinctively drawn to her every word. "I listened as best as I could. Gwen told me about the two girls—Eleanor and Genevieve. She described how Eleanor had locked Genevieve in the Zeppelin and left her behind. It was hard to hear, watching her lie there, knowing she didn't have much time left. But her eyes were wide, holding me with such intensity, I couldn't look away. She made me promise to remember."

The girls were silent, taking in the weight of Gwen's last words. Larissa broke the quiet.

"So… she told you about us?" she asked, her voice barely above a whisper.

Mary nodded, her expression somber. "Yes. She told me your names. She said Milda would have the ability to move things, that Larissa would have the gift of sight, like her, and that Kate… Kate would be able to heal." Mary paused, glancing at Kate. "I didn't realize she was talking about you. You never showed any abilities when you were here, though, with all the trouble you had with the other kids, I see it now. One of the girls mentioned that you made a little boy sick, but that you fixed him. At the time, I just thought she was trying to get you into trouble."

Kate's face flushed with heat. She remembered that day with the boy, but she didn't acknowledge it.

Mary picked up the photo and turned it over, rubbing her fingers along the edges. "Gwen also told me that you three would come to my door, with a dog," she said, motioning to Bob. "And that I was to tell you everything she had told me."

The girls sat back, overwhelmed by the revelation. Larissa spoke up, her voice quiet but firm.

"So what does this picture and Gwen have to do with us?"

Mary placed the photo down on the table, closer to the girls. "I'm not entirely sure. But Gwen always referred to you three as her sisters.

Kate glanced at Larissa, who dropped her head and looked away, her eyes were glossy. She turned back to Mary. "Wait, Gwen was here eleven years before I was. I came when I was five, but Gwen was here when she was thirteen. That would mean… she'd be forty-two by now."

Milda whistled low. "Wow, that's old! Or would be…"

Kate frowned, shaking her head. "But that doesn't make sense. It's already hard to believe the three of us are sisters. How could Gwen be our sister too? There's a twenty-one-year age gap between me and her."

Mary placed the cross back in its box and sighed. "I thought it was because you all shared a special gift, so she referred to you as sister like or something. There's more to the story, but Gwen was fading fast. In her last moments, she said 'our mother,' and she reached for the picture. She grabbed the left side, and I think she was trying to tell me that Eleanor was her mother. But she said 'our,' so maybe she was referring to you three as well."

Milda sat up quickly, making Bob jump. "Wait… that's our mother?" She grabbed the picture, studying it closely. "Which one?"

Mary tapped the left side of the photo. "The one on the left. The smudge in the corner was where Gwen was trying to point."

Milda stared at the picture in her hands. "What the heck did Gwen have all over her hands? She almost ruined the whole picture… the picture of my mom!"

Larissa leaned in, her voice low. "That's Gwen's blood, Milda."

Milda recoiled, horrified. She threw the photo back onto the desk, and it fluttered to the ground. Kate picked it up, holding it out to Mary.

"Thank you," Kate said softly. "This… is a lot to take in. But I think we have more questions now than we did before we came here."

Mary smiled faintly. "Yes, I figured you would. You can keep the picture. I think Gwen would have wanted you to have it." She stood and carefully placed the box back on its shelf. Turning to face the girls, she opened the bottom left drawer of her desk and began rummaging through it.

"A couple of years later, I came across a newspaper article about a candy shop opening. I was drawn back to the picture several times, so I cut it out and kept it on my desk. For weeks, I couldn't figure out why it looked so familiar. Ah, here it is." Mary pulled out a newspaper clipping and laid it on the table between the girls.

Milda snatched it up eagerly. "Hey, that's our mom!"

Larissa leaned closer to get a better look. Kate squinted at the image, her thoughts swirling. "That can't be our mom. She looks barely older than I am, and Mary said it was just a few years after Gwen died." Kate looked from the photo to the newspaper clipping. "But this girl… she's the spitting image of Eleanor. Do you think it's her daughter?"

"I think it might be," Mary said, her voice steady. "And I bet she will have more answers for you. If Gwen meant actual sisters, then she's likely your sister too."

For the next twenty minutes they all took turns trying to guess what had happened, eventually exhausting all scenarios. As the girls said their goodbyes, Mary promised she would go through the attic and see if there were any personal belongings of Gwen's that may help them.

Thirteen

Carol's lie

Milda and Larissa had decided during the car ride home that they would visit the candy store. Milda was very enthusiastic and relentless in her determination to go. They'd finally convinced Kate to join them, though she still wasn't sure whether it was the mystery of the lady in the photo possibly being their mother or the allure of the candy driving Milda's excitement. On their way across town, John had called to say dinner would be a little late, his meeting was running behind, but he expected them to be there. None of them could come up with a believable excuse that wouldn't raise suspicion with him, and since they weren't keen on bringing him along, they went home for chicken and mashed potatoes, postponing the candy store visit until the next day.

John and the girls had arrived home at almost the exact same time. Larissa and Milda were in the kitchen getting a snack. Milda could not wait another minute for something to eat, while John had gone to change his clothes and wash up before starting to make dinner. Kate was opening the curtains to let the afternoon sun in.

It was a bright afternoon, the sun hanging low enough in the sky to cast long shadows along the sidewalk. Kate stood at the dining room window of their third-floor apartment, holding both the curtains that she had just opened in her hands still. Her eyes tracing the figures across the street. There, near the corner of the alley, stood Dillan and Carol. They were standing a little too close, their body language tense. Kate couldn't make out the words from this distance, but the way Dillan's posture was stiff, the way Carol's hands were gesturing sharply, it didn't sit right with her.

She squinted, trying to make sense of the exchange. The more she watched, the more it seemed like they knew each other—too well. Kate had never seen Dillan this animated, especially not in a conversation with someone like Carol. It was unsettling. Dillan was always calm, collected, like he wasn't entirely of this world. Carol, on the other hand… she had a way of acting like she belonged in every corner of the room. But this? This didn't feel right.

Then, as if on cue, Carol turned and walked briskly toward the building, disappearing into the front door. Kate blinked, rubbing her eyes. Maybe she was just reading too much into it, but the whole thing felt off.

Moments later, Carol knocked on the apartment door, and Kate's heart skipped. She opened it, forcing a smile as Carol stepped inside.

"Hey, Carol," Kate said, trying to sound casual, even though the questions were bubbling up inside her.

"Hi, Kate," Carol replied, her voice smooth, her smile almost too rehearsed. "I hope I'm not interrupting. I was invited by your dad to join you all for dinner."

"Oh, no, of course not," Kate said, stepping aside to let her in. "He just got back from his meeting, so we're all pitching in to get dinner ready."

As Carol made her way into the kitchen, Kate followed, keeping an eye on her. It was hard not to feel a little suspicious, given what she'd just witnessed. It was just too odd—the way Carol had walked off after the conversation with Dillan and then showed up here. But Kate was careful not to show any of this.

Soon enough, dinner preparations were underway. Larissa and Milda were setting the table, while John and Kate worked on the dishes. Carol, ever the social one, offered to help with the salad and even cracked a few jokes to lighten the mood. It almost felt normal, but Kate couldn't shake the odd sense that something was wrong.

Milda had managed to turn one of the place mats into a makeshift hat. She was standing at the counter, balancing a spoon on her nose.

"Look, I'm a wizard," she said, her voice muffled by the spoon. "Do you want to know what's on the menu? A magical feast of… mashed potatoes and more mashed potatoes!"

Larissa rolled her eyes. "You're going to be a magician, huh? Are you sure you don't want to start with a career in clowning?"

"Hey, there's an art to it," Milda said seriously, "One day, you'll all see."

Carol, who had been silently observing, couldn't help but chuckle. "I don't think I've seen anyone juggle silverware quite like that."

Milda paused, considering the challenge. "You mean… like this?" she said, attempting to toss a fork and knife into the air. They clattered to the floor.

Everyone paused, and then John sighed dramatically. "Let's just stick to setting the table, huh?"

Milda grinned and gave a mock bow. "Fine, fine. But I'll be back for my magic act later."

When everyone finally sat down at the dinner table, with the scent of freshly roasted chicken filling the air, Kate decided to bring it up. She couldn't ignore it anymore.

"So…" Kate said casually, glancing at Carol before turning to her dad. "The other day, when we were at the deli, I couldn't help but feel like you and Dillan knew each other. Is that weird?" Her voice was calm, but her eyes were sharp, watching Carol's reaction closely.

Carol paused mid-bite, her fork hovering in the air. For a moment, she didn't say anything, and Kate's heart raced as she waited for her answer.

"Dillan? No, I would remember if we had met before. That was the first time we had met at the Deli with you," Carol replied smoothly, a little too smoothly. She put her fork down, almost too deliberately, and smiled.

Kate studied her, her intuition gnawing at her. Something didn't add up, but she couldn't quite put her finger on it. Before she could press further, John cleared his throat, and the conversation shifted to lighter topics.

As the evening wore on, Kate kept a close eye on Carol, wondering if the unease she felt was just her overthinking, or if there was something deeper at play.

Fourteen

Road trip

Early the next morning, John left for the orphanage to try out some of the old hardware he had salvaged. Milda, ever watchful, saw his truck turn the corner and immediately signaled to Larissa. The girls bolted from the house, Bob racing them down the stairs. Milda had insisted they be on their way as soon as John left, which meant Kate was skipping breakfast.

Kate put the car in drive and headed towards the interstate. She wasn't entirely sure what she was doing, but at least she had a direction. Lately, her life had been shrouded in mystery. Now, however, she was piecing together clues from her past. She was excited, but a lingering fear gnawed at her, one she would never admit to—fear for the safety of her new sisters. She glanced at the two of them in the rear view mirror. Both were singing along to the song on the radio, while Bob, the moose of a dog, shook his head in time with the music. Kate turned onto the interstate, merging into traffic.

Milda caught her eye in the rear view mirror. "Hey, how long is this going to take?"

"It'll be about an hour."

"That's forever!"

"Well, just sit back and relax, and we'll be there before you know it." Kate smirked, mimicking her dad's typical line on road trips. She wasn't sure how John would react to her decision to go without him, but for now, it felt right—just the three of them, learning their past and connecting the dots. Kate wondered if maybe she should have waited for him.

"No, you did the right thing." Larissa's voice cut through the music, and she went right back to singing.

"You know, that's going to get really annoying."

"You have no idea!" Larissa giggled.

"Could you maybe keep the comments to yourself?" Kate tried to sound stern, but a part of her appreciated that Larissa seemed genuinely concerned about their situation, especially for a thirteen-year-old.

"Yep, I could," Larissa said, glancing up at the rear view mirror.

"But you're not going to, are you?" Kate winked.

Larissa smiled and returned to her singing. Milda, who had started singing louder, drowned out Kate's voice. Bob looked at Kate in the mirror, winked at her, and returned to swaying along with the music.

"Did Bob just wink at me?" Kate asked, turning around to look at the dog.

Bob leaned forward and licked her from the bottom of her chin to her bangs.

"Ugh! Gross, dog breath!" Kate turned back to the road, wiping the slobber off with her sleeve.

"What did you feed that dog? It smells like liver and onions!" Kate pulled out a napkin from the glove box. She always kept napkins in the glove box for emergencies.

"How long?" Milda bounced up and down in the seat. "I can't hold it anymore!"

Kate glanced into the rear view mirror. "We left 15 minutes ago. You went before we left. There's no way you need to go already."

Bob sitting between the two girls in the back seemed interested in something behind them and let out a low growl.

"There's a rest stop in a mile." Larissa added, still gazing out the window. Bob continued to concentrate on what was behind them and started to whimper.

"I have to go really bad, and Bob does too!" Milda crossed her legs, continuing to bounce.

"We'll never get there if we have to stop every twenty minutes!" Kate maneuvered the car into the right lane, scanning for a rest stop. Bob whimpered again, hopping around with Milda.

"I'm looking for a place, but your bouncing is very distracting," Kate muttered, her eyes still on the road.

Larissa turned to face forward. "You're missing the exit."

Kate shot a glance at Larissa in the mirror. "I'm not going to miss it! The last sign said exit 42 is the rest stop, and we're—" Her eyes widened. "Shit!"

She yanked the steering wheel right, just making it onto exit 42. Milda slid into Bob, who slid into Larissa, causing her to grunt. Kate slammed on the brakes, slowing the car to the posted speed limit, and pulled into the first available spot. Milda flung the door open and bolted toward the bathroom. Bob leapt from the seat and bound out as well.

Kate jumped out and followed Milda, calling, "Hey, you can't just take off running like that!"

Milda ignored her, throwing her hand back and speeding toward the women's restroom. Kate jogged up just in time to see Milda slam into the bathroom door. "Well, I guess she really had to go!"

Kate checked the map on the kiosk while she waited, eyeing the people coming and going. She snickered at an older man in spandex shorts, black socks, and white sneakers. As she watched him walk away the same black bird from the courtyard flew by. Kate watched it fly through the trees and land looking back at her.

Milda appeared at her side and put her hand in Kates.

"Eww, your hand is wet!" Kate yanked her hand away and wiped it on her jeans. "There weren't any paper towels in the bathroom!"

Milda, oblivious, started wiping her hands on the back of Kate's jeans.

Kate shot her a look of disbelief.

"What?" she said, following Kate toward the car.

"I swear, Milda, use your own jeans!" Milda grabbed Kate's hand again and they started towards the car. Kate glanced back over her shoulder to look for the bird, but it was gone.

Fifteen

The perfect spy

As Larissa sat in the car waiting for everyone to return, she had a sense about her. Instinctively she turned slightly so that she could just see the backward reflection in the rear-view mirror. Larissa moved her head back and forth trying to use the mirror to see what might be drawing her attention.

After a moment she spotted it, about five parking spots back. She could just make out one of the shady characters Dillan had been talking with at the sandwich shop. It was Kris. It looked like she was waiting. Clearly, she had been following them and was hanging out waiting for them to resume the trip.

As she kept an eye on Kris, Bob trotted into view. He went straight up to the car and put his front paws on the driver's side window. The window rolled down. Larissa shuttered. From her view it looked like they were talking.

Why hadn't she seen this?

As she continued to watch, Bob turned quickly, looking in her direction. Larissa moved her head so as not to be caught looking back in the mirror.

Kate and Milda returned to the car, Milda jumping into the back seat. "Where's Bob?"

Kate was still coming around the front of the car, Larissa lowered her voice and talked fast.

"That girl, Kris, from the sandwich shop is following us, and Bob just went over and it looked like he was talking to her!"

Milda jerked around to see, Larissa grabbed her down. "Don't Look!"

"But why? Do you think Bob is her dog?"

"No, I think Bob is a spy."

"First, she's talking with Dillan, now Bob." Milda was still trying to peak over the back of the seat, "You know we have never seen Bob and Dillan at the same time… Maybe Dillan is Bob!"

Larissa quickly "we need to just pretend like everything is fine until we know more"

Kate had reached her door, and getting in she noticed the girls whispering. "What's going on back there? Bob isn't back yet. I am not chasing after him, he can just stay here."

Milda under her breath, "that might not be a bad idea"

Bob came running up to the car and jumped in next to Milda.

Milda could not resist and whispered in Bob's ear, "We saw you, we know what you were doing."

Bob twisted his head, his eyes looked like he was pleading with her. He looked at Larissa, then back to Milda, let out a loud bark and licked Milda across the mouth. Bob continued to lick, taking turns between Milda and Larissa's' cheeks.

"Okay, Okay, I am sure you had a good reason!" Larissa said and pulled Bob's face away. Bob gave out two more loud barks and then settled between the two girls, a paw on both of their laps.

Kate turned around to look at them. "You know, if I didn't know any better, I'd swear Bob knows exactly what we're saying. It's like he is almost human." Milda and Larissa looked at each other and started petting Bob, who gave out a small whimper.

Kate reached over and helped Milda buckle into her seat. Bob seized the opportunity to lick Kate across the cheek, her nose, and her chin.

"Hey! Come on!" Kate grabbed another napkin from the glove box and wiped the dog slobber from her face.

"Okay, are we all set?" Kate asked as she dropped the napkin in the passenger seat, then put the car in reverse. "I have no idea what made me think this was a good idea."

She backed out of the parking spot and headed back to the interstate. Behind them, another car was doing the same.

Sixteen

The candy shop

The rest of the interstate trip was uneventful. Kate found the exit and made the turn with plenty of time, continuing down a few streets and then taking a left on State Avenue. Milda sat in the back, holding the newspaper clipping, peering out the window, trying to spot the storefront from the picture. Larissa sat beside her; eyes closed. Kate watched them in the rear view mirror.

"Larissa? What's wrong? Are you seeing something?" Kate asked, her voice soft.

"No," Larissa replied, not moving.

"Why do you look so sad—well, sadder than usual, anyway?" Kate adjusted the mirror to get a better look at Larissa's face. Bob dropped his head into Larissa's lap, and she absentmindedly petted him.

"I'm fine. Everything will be fine," Larissa said, opening her eyes and staring out the front window. "Next block, turn left, second store on the right." Larissa closed her eyes again.

Kate chuckled. "I don't think I'll ever get used to that."

"I love that she can see the future!" Milda started bouncing up and down in her seat. They were getting close.

Kate turned the corner slowly, squinting through the windshield.

Milda jumped forward point ahead, "Hey! That looks like Carol." A figure was slipping into the candy shop, with a very familiar frame.

"It is Carol." Larissa said, not moving.

Kate coasted past the storefront, catching a quick glimpse of Carol disappearing behind the counter, the *Closed* sign flipped firmly in place. No candy trays out. No lights on in the displays.

Kate's grip on the steering wheel tightened. "That was Carol."

Kate's doubts about Carol came rushing back.

She pulled into the alley by the candy shop and parked. "Stay here," she told the girls and Bob. "All of you."

"But—" Milda started.

"No. Stay in the car."

Kate's voice brokered no argument. The door clicked shut behind her.

At the front of the shop she tested the handle, Unlocked.

The bell didn't jingle as she eased the door open. Inside, the shop was cold, still. The scent of artificial vanilla lingered like a lie. She moved quietly, hearing muffled voices beyond the back hallway.

"...Why do they have to die?" It was Carol's voice, uncharacteristically small, uncertain.

"You know why!" another voice snapped. Cold, sharp. Familiar without ever being heard before.

Kate moved down the hall, heart pounding.

"But can't I just... be your daughter?" Carol said, pleading now. "Not a spy, not a weapon. I don't want to kill my best friend."

Kate stopped cold.

Carol's voice broke. "Please."

There was a silence that dragged like a knife. Then: *rumbling*. The walls trembled faintly. Kate pressed against the wall, breath shallow. Her mind reeled. Carol? Her best friend? Sent to kill her?

Then, a sudden stillness.

"Kate," the cold voice called, loud and clear. "Why don't you come back here and join us?"

Kate spun, intending to run, but the display counters she'd passed earlier shuddered violently, slammed together, and surged down the hallway behind her, boxing her in.

Nowhere to go.

She took a breath and stepped forward into the warehouse.

It was cavernous, stark, and industrial—metal scaffolding, crates stacked high, pallets, shadows. Not a trace of candy anywhere. Just steel and secrets. Carol stood to one side; eyes wide, frozen in horror.

And the woman in the center—tall, commanding, wrapped in black and silver—smiled at Kate like a wolf with a secret.

"Thank you for coming," Eleanor said. "I am so pleased that I get to be the one to tell you myself. You see, Carol has a secret. I don't know, maybe it would be better if you told her Carol?"

Carol lowered her head and looked away. Not able to face either one of them.

Eleanor continued with disgust in her voice. "Just as I thought, soft through and through. You see Kate... Carol was placed in your life to draw your mother out. To help me find the others. And now, she has a final task."

Eleanor turned to her daughter. "Prove yourself, child. Kill her."

Carol shook her head. "I can't. I *won't*."

Seventeen

A family reunion

Back in the alley, the scene in the car was tense.

"I really have to pee," Milda whispered, jiggling in her seat.

"Hold it," Larissa said, eyes still fixed on the candy shop's front.

Milda wasn't good at holding anything—not questions, not secrets, and definitely not her bladder. She spotted a side door halfway down the alley, a quick jog from the car. Without warning, she threw the door open and jumped out.

"Milda—!" Larissa snapped, fumbling with her seat belt.

But Bob was already out too, tail wagging, tongue lolling.

"I have to Pee!" Milda scurried to the door and reached up, stretching. "Ugh, the handle's too high. Lari!"

Larissa caught up, huffing. "You can't just run off like that."

"But I *really* have to—wait, have you seen this?" Milda pointed at the old door, its paint chipping in long flakes. "It's kinda cool. Mysterious."

"Yeah," Larissa said flatly. "It's a door."

She reached up and twisted the handle. The door creaked open with a groan that echoed into the alley way, leaving the girls with an eerie feeling.

Larissa glanced down at her sister. "Please stay with me. And be quiet for just a bit. *Both* of you," she added, giving Bob a look. Bob wagged his tail, oblivious.

They stepped inside.

The hallway was dim and lined with dusty office doors on either side. Old blinds hung crooked, and the air smelled like cardboard and floor wax. Milda bounced down the hall, cracking open each door hopefully.

"Bathroom?"

"Nope."

"Bathroom?"

"Definitely not."

"Ooh, this one has a weird chair in it."

"Focus," Larissa whispered harshly. "We're not here for—"

Voices.

They froze.

Somewhere ahead—beyond the hall, through a wider opening—they could hear a woman's voice. Low, commanding. Angry.

Another voice, shaking.

Carol.

"I don't want to kill my best friend."

The words froze the air in Larissa's lungs.

Milda stopped jiggling, eyes going wide.

The hallway opened ahead. Larissa inched forward, careful to stay close to the wall. Milda tiptoed behind her, Bob's nails tapping softly on the concrete floor.

They reached the edge of the warehouse space, peering around the corner just in time to hear Carol say, clearly and firmly:

"I can't. I won't."

Milda forgetting all about the bathroom moved forward for a better assessment of the situation. "You won't what?"

"Kill your sister, Kate" Eleanor says harshly, never taking her eyes off Carol.

Kate moves quickly towards the girls. Larissa, Milda and Bob follow suite and meet in the middle, with Carol and Eleanor forming the other two sides of a tense triangle.

"Really, what the fu..! Hey, you're Eleanor!" Milda stopped and stared, wide-eyed. "Are you our mom?"

Milda's question hung in the air.

"No Milda, I am not your mother" Eleanor was now assessing the girls as they came to a stop together.

"How did you know my name?" Milda asked.

"She can see the future, too," Larissa said, her tone matter of fact.

"That's right," Eleanor agreed, focusing on Larissa. "Which tells me you're the seer in the bunch."

Larissa didn't respond right away but instead gave Eleanor a guarded look. "Yes, I can," she said, her voice a little rougher than usual.

"And you still came?" Eleanor's gaze hardened, fixating on Larissa.

Kate turned her head slightly so she could face Larissa but still keep Eleanor in her peripheral. "What does she mean, we still came? What haven't you told me?"

Eleanor and Larissa held eye contact for a moment longer before Eleanor finally looked at Kate. "She didn't tell you because she's learned not to try to change the future. You have to accept it and make the best of it. That's the curse of seeing," she said, her tone almost apologetic.

Kate blinked, processing the weight of Eleanor's words. "Wait, you saw this coming?"

Eleanor turned to Milda, her expression softening but grinning like a scary clown. "So, let's see. What's your special talent?"

"I can make stuff fly!" Milda grinned, excited by the question, then paused, her excitement dampening as she realized something. "Hey, are you our sister? It would be the coolest thing to have a sister with a candy shop!"

"I'm not your sister," Eleanor said, her voice turning serious.

Larissa continued in Eleanor's silence. "She was our mother's best friend… and she tried to kill her."

"You knew she was not our mother, and you still let us come here?" Kate's voice rose with disbelief.

Before Kate could continue, Eleanor cut in, her voice measured but firm. "Like I said, Larissa has learned not to mess with fate. I imagine she has tried before—hell, so would I. But it only makes things worse, not better. You must accept it, as she has. And she brought you to me."

Eleanor turned and began pacing slowly behind some small crates. "Perhaps before we get started, you'd like to know about your mother?"

"Get what started?" Milda said not catching on. Larissa held a hand in front of Milda's mouth.

Eleanor gave a small grin and continued.

"Your sister is right. I am Eleanor, and your mother and I were the best of friends. Our families were close, inseparable," Eleanor said, leaning against a crate.

"The special powers we possess are passed down through either the father or the mother. If both parents have powers, their children are often very powerful, sometimes possessing more than one ability."

Eleanor paused for a moment before continuing, her voice becoming more somber. "About three thousand years ago, children from two very powerful families but different races."

Eleanor turns and looks at them directly, "I am sorry I can't go into more detail about the races, we don't have all night"

Continuing, "the Children, who were very spoiled, and mostly evil, decided they wanted to rule, there were, two brothers and a sister. Naturally, the rest of the families resisted. The fighting lasted almost a 100 years before the children and all of their relatives were destroyed. That left two other families with powers in charge: One was of the Nidteran race, and the other was of the Raverine race.

Larissa cut in, her voice steady. "Our mother is Nidteran, our father was Raverine."

"That's right," Eleanor agreed, her voice barely a whisper.

"For centuries, our families lived and ruled without any problems, until about eighty-three years ago, when your mother and my brother fell in love." Eleanor shook her head slightly. "They kept it a secret for many years—even from me. I still don't know how we didn't see it coming."

Eleanor stopped and took a deep breath before continuing. "One day, your mother came to me. She was upset. She confessed that she and my brother were in love, but worst of all, she was pregnant."

"Wait, what?" Milda interrupted, her voice full of shock. "You're saying Mom was pregnant?"

"Yes," Eleanor confirmed, her tone growing tense. "Because of what had happened in the past, there was strict laws that no persons with powers from the opposite races could have children, it was too risky. The punishment was death— for both of them.

Eleanor's voice started to shake with emotion, but she quickly regained composure. "She told me their plan—they were going to run away. They'd already arranged passage, and my husband, Alexander, and several of our closest friends were helping them. Your mother asked me to go with them. Of course I did, we were the best of friends, like sisters."

Eleanor paused, lost in thought for a moment before she continued. "But the day we were supposed to leave, everything went wrong. Someone had told some of the council members. We all gathered at the meeting spot anyways, but your father didn't show up. We had a short window to leave; Alexander went to find him. But he didn't return, your father did instead. He told us that Alexander, had been stabbed and was dead." Eleanor paused. No one made a sound.

We had to leave. We couldn't stay, not with everything going wrong, so we left. As we were heading to the portal one of the council guards caught site of us. Your father was fatally injured and stayed behind to give us a better chance of making it."

Eleanor walked over to a desk on the wall and picked up a photo. "This is a picture of your mother, my Alexander in the middle, and your father Jedrek." Eleanor, realizing no one was moving, put the picture on a crate about halfway between them and went back to where she had been leaning.

Milda ran over and grabbed the picture, looking at it as she returned to her sisters. "Hey, they look exactly alike!" she said, wide-eyed.

"They were twins," Eleanor said quietly from behind them.

"Okay, so now we know you." Milda pointing a finger at Eleanor. "Aaaand you're crazy." Pausing for emphasis. "And we now know who my dad is, uh was…"

Milda started flipping the picture in her hand. She quickly pivoted, staring directly at Carol.

"So why is Carol here?" she asked, puzzled.

"Was she, like… buying candy?"

The warehouse fell into a heavy, dreadful silence.

Eleanor turned her gaze to Milda, lips curling into something cruel.

"Oh, silly child. Carol isn't *just* here."

She took a slow step forward, the shadows around her pulsing like a heartbeat.

"I planted Carol years ago, woven into Kate's life like a weed disguised as a flower. Not because I needed a spy. No… I needed bait."

Kate tensed, looking at Carol and then quickly looking away, fists clenched.

Eleanor continued, "You see, your mother—*Genevieve*—was hiding. And what better way to draw out a coward than to dangle her children in front of her? One by one. I had to find you all and make sure she knew that I was hunting you."

Milda blinked. "Wait. *We* were the bait. That's messed up."

Eleanor ignored her.

"Carol's job was simple," she said, with a casual shrug. "Become close. Gain trust. Learn the truth. And when the time came—kill you all. Quick. Clean. Efficient."

Larissa, from the side of the room, called out, "She didn't do it, though. So that kind of makes her a terrible assassin."

Milda, nodding solemnly, added, "Yeah, like… zero stars. Would not recommend."

Eleanor's smile cracked with irritation. "She *was* supposed to be my masterpiece. My own daughter—crafted to be a perfect tool."

Milda, tilting her head: "Wait. Carol's your *actual* daughter? Like nine months and out she came, child?"

Eleanor, coldly: "Biological. Not that it matters now. She's become… defective."

Kate stood slowly, shifting a bit to put herself between Carol and Eleanor.

"She's not a tool. She's a person."

Milda, talking sideways to Larissa: "This is getting really confusing, right?"

Larissa, dry: "Yeah, and we haven't even gotten to the 'long-lost brother' part yet."

Milda, "Yeah… Wait? What?"

"Enough! Now you know, now… you die." Eleanor started flailing her arms around.

A massive crate lifted into the air from behind her, floating with impossible ease. Then it flew straight at Kate.

Larissa threw out both hands, as if she knew, catching the crate mid-air with a shuddering blast of her own power, sending it crashing harmlessly to the side.

"Stay here," she told Milda, but Milda was already moving.

Larissa sprinted forward; eyes locked on Eleanor. Her vision was flaring colors and shifting, time was slowing for her. She could *feel* the energy moving in the air, the currents that fed Eleanor's fury. A ripple in the world.

Another crate rose.

Larissa reached out instinctively—*and caught it in midair.*

Her own powers surged, raw and bright, forming a shimmering aura around her hand as she twisted the crate's momentum and slammed it into the floor before it could reach anyone else.

Eleanor's gaze snapped to her. "Oh," she said darkly. "Another one."

From behind, Milda shrieked—not in fear, but excitement. "Did you *see* that?! Lari! You're like a Jedi!"

Bob lunged at Eleanor with a sharp bark, teeth bared.

With a simple wave, Eleanor threw Bob crashing into the shelves lining the wall.

Bob let out a yelp.

"Bob!" Milda screamed running to his side.

"Milda!" Larissa yelled, already raising her hands again. Another crate was launching their way. "I need help!"

"OKAY!" Milda ducked behind a metal barrel sitting next to Bob. With a strange kind of confidence, flung out both hands. The barrel skidded forward as if nudged by invisible hands—awkward, slow—but moving.

Eleanor sneered. "Children playing with matches."

She raised both arms, calling more objects into the air—tools, chairs, whole tables spinning wildly above them.

She called out. "Carol! Let's finish this!"

Carol was just standing there, unsure what to do, as the warehouse was turning into a battlefield.

Larissa stepped forward again, steadying her breath, meeting Eleanor's eyes, but also watching Carol.

Eleanor, realizing Carol was of no help, decided to sprint back further into the warehouse for better cover.

Larissa pulled the shelves behind Eleanor down, not on top of Eleanor, but behind her, blocking her exit.

Milda had joined in, although slowly, she thru a couple crates on top of the broken shelves.

"Are you kidding me? Do you really want to play like that?" Eleanor yelled, clearly pissed.

"Sorry!" Milda shouted. "Not really," she whispered and giggled.

Eleanor's hair began to float up, her face turning red with rage. The crates in front of them started to shake.

"This is not going to be good, is it?" Kate asked.

"Nope, this is going to get bad," Larissa said, her voice tense.

"Now what?" Kate asked, looking around.

"Run!" Milda and Larissa said together.

As the girls started to run for the far side of the warehouse, a crate flew into the air, landing twenty feet ahead of them. They pulled up short, shielding their faces.

"It's not going to be that easy!" Eleanor screamed across the room.

"We're going to have to stand and fight," Larissa said, kicking a piece of wood off her shoe.

"Fighting sounds like fun!" Milda threw her fists up.

"We're not going to get anywhere near her!" Kate said, placing a hand on Milda's shoulder and pulling her back.

"Milda, get mad!" Larissa said. "It's time to let the rage out! That woman tried to kill your mom, and she hurt Bob"

Milda looked over at Bob lying lifeless on the ground. Her hair started to rise, her face glowing as red as Eleanor's. "No one hurts my Dog!"

Several crates to the left of Eleanor rose into the air, flying toward her. Eleanor raised her hand, and the crates flew to the side.

"You're going to have to try a little harder, little one. This isn't playtime," Eleanor sneered.

"I'm just getting warmed up!" Milda yelled back. Several boxes on the right flew at Eleanor. She ducked and motioned them into the side wall, where they exploded.

"Better! But you need to work on your aim," Eleanor taunted, toying with them.

"I'm not sure what we're going to do. Whatever we try, she blocks." Kate kept her eyes on Eleanor but noticed Larissa was staring blankly ahead, her eyes closed and her body very still.

"Lari?" Kate asked, her voice tight. She couldn't pull her eyes from the scene of danger ahead, but she was starting to get worried about Larissa.

"Lari!" Kate called, now panicking. She had brought them here. They were her responsibility, and this wasn't how she had planned it.

"Shh. I'm concentrating." Larissa's voice barely moved her lips, but it was enough to calm Kate's nerves, even just a little. Kate refocused, her attention snapping back to Eleanor just as Eleanor grabbed her ears, wincing in pain.

"Get out of my head, you little witch! Your mother used to do that to me when I was a kid! I hated it then, and I hate it now!" Eleanor screamed, swinging her arms around. A crate on the floor flew toward Larissa.

Milda immediately moved in front of Larissa, raising her arms. The crate hovered in mid-air, struggling against their combined powers.

Larissa kept her concentration, pushing further into Eleanor's mind.

The crate dropped to the ground as Eleanor clutched her head, muttering to herself. She looked up, her hair raising, eyes glowing with a red intensity. The ground rumbled, and the air grew thick, making it harder to breathe.

"This can't be good!" Kate shouted over the rising noise. Tremors shook the floor beneath them. Kate widened her stance, keeping her balance while making sure Larissa and Milda wouldn't fall. When she placed her hands on their shoulders, the air seemed to settle. Energy sparked in Kate's chest.

"Wow, what did you do? My thoughts are clearer now!" Larissa turned toward Kate, releasing Eleanor from her mind momentarily.

"Hey! That kind of tickles!'" Milda laughed, also feeling the surge of energy, which made it much easier to move the crate she had just been battling with.

Kate strengthened her grip on the girls, "Alright, I think it is time you two kicked her ass!"

"Oh! You said 'ass!'" Milda turned her head around, wagging her finger at Kate.

"Hey! Concentrate!" Kate said, and Milda immediately spun back around, looking for the next crate to throw at Eleanor.

Eleanor looked like she was losing her edge. With Larissa's playing in her head and Milda's growing rage, they were pushing her back. Eleanor was in pain but refused to give up. The rumbling continued, shaking the building, and the girls swayed with every tremor.

Milda planted her feet firmly, her small body trembling with both fear and fury. "You can't kill us. You're not going to win!"

"Watch me," Eleanor sneered, but her words were tainted with uncertainty. The tides were turning, and the girls could feel it. This wasn't just a fight for survival anymore; it was a fight for what was right.

Eleanor's eyes blazed, her energy surging outward with a snap. A heavy metal crate from the far side of the room trembled, then launched itself through the air like a missile—out of view of the girls, straight toward Milda.

"No!" Carol screamed, finally coming alive.

She thrust out both hands, her power flaring, intercepting the crate just before it could strike Milda. The impact of Carol's shield cracked through the air, sending shock waves that knocked papers and debris into the air. The crate clattered to the ground, dented but harmless.

Everyone froze.

Milda blinked up at Carol in shock. Larissa moved closer, shielding her sister instinctively, while Kate stared, her emotions a war zone of betrayal and confusion.

Eleanor stepped forward slowly, eyes narrowing. "What are you doing?"

Carol was trembling, but she didn't move away. Her voice wavered at first but steadied with every word. "Stopping you."

"You're protecting them?" Eleanor sneered, her voice sharp with disbelief. "After everything I've done for you. After everything we've planned together?"

Carol's jaw clenched. "You raised me to be loyal. To be ruthless. You taught me how to lie, manipulate, and win. And I believed you. I did everything you asked—"

"You *owe* me!" Eleanor barked.

Carol shook her head, tears welling up in her eyes. "No, I *believed* you. That's different. I believed you when you said this was the only way. That power was everything. That Kate's family had to die. But you were wrong."

Eleanor's face twitched with fury. "I made you who you are."

Carol stepped closer, placing herself squarely between Eleanor and the others. "You made me someone I don't want to be. I came into Kate's life thinking I was on a mission. Just another step in your plan. But she treated me like family. She trusted me. *They* trusted me."

Her voice cracked. "Kate is my best friend. She was never supposed to mean anything to me—but she does. And I can't stand here and let you kill her. Or Milda. Or Larissa. I won't."

The silence that followed was razor-sharp. Kate stared at Carol, heart pounding. Her mind wanted to push her away, to scream that none of this made up for the lies—but her gut told her the truth was in Carol's voice. Raw. Real.

Eleanor's expression twisted, hatred blooming like wildfire. "You ungrateful child."

Carol didn't flinch. "I'd rather be ungrateful than become you."

Eleanor's power surged again, shadows rippling around her like smoke. "Then you'll fall with them."

"No," Carol whispered, steeling herself. "I'll stand with them."

Eleanor's fury exploded into motion. The walls trembled with the force of her anger. Power lashed out, chaotic and uncontrolled, aimed now not just at the girls—but at her own daughter.

Kate pulled Milda back, shielding her again as Larissa braced for another attack. But Carol stood her ground, power rising in her hands, ready to defend the very people she was sent to destroy.

It was no longer mother versus daughter. It was belief versus blood.

Eleanor screamed—an unearthly, guttural sound that shattered the air. Her fury turned into motion, into violence. She ripped through the warehouse with her power, tearing crates, metal piping, and shattered glass from every surface and hurling them at the girls with frightening speed.

"Get down!" Larissa yelled, diving behind a toppled worktable.

Carol spun in place, throwing up shields of shimmering energy, catching two crates midair and slamming them harmlessly to the ground. Milda flung out her hand and a large coil of wire sprang from a shelf, whipping through the air toward Eleanor.

Eleanor caught it effortlessly, twisting the metal with a flick of her wrist and sending it flying back like a spear. Milda ducked just in time, scrambling behind a support pillar.

Debris rained around them—glass, sharp metal, broken wooden frames. Carol was everywhere, spinning, blocking, shielding. She had become their front line, protecting them from Eleanor's storm of rage.

A metal wrench slipped past her defenses.

It sliced through the air and hurtled towards Larissa.

Carol's head snapped toward the sound of it—too late to stop it—but Larissa managed to duck, the wrench grazing her arm and embedding into the wall behind her.

"Are you okay?" Carol gasped, turning her back to Eleanor for just a moment.

That was all it took.

A steel beam ripped from the ceiling and shot forward, slamming into Carol's side with brutal force. It struck her like a hammer, knocking her off her feet and pinning her to the ground beneath it with a sickening thud.

"Carol!" Kate screamed, racing toward her.

Eleanor's eyes widened for just a heartbeat—just long enough for devastation to flicker across her features. "No..." she whispered.

But then the old fury returned. She hardened. She turned away.

And ran.

Eleanor disappeared through a side door, her cloak billowing behind her, vanishing into the night as the remaining debris settled in eerie silence.

The girls rushed to Carol's side.

"Carol? Hey! Carol!" Kate dropped to her knees, her hands shaking as she touched her friend's face.

Carol winced, barely conscious, but her mouth curled into a lopsided smirk. "Sooo... am I still invited to Christmas Dinner?"

Milda choked out a laugh through her tears. "we'll let you know."

Then Carol's eyes fluttered, her body going slack. She passed out.

"Move," Milda said, planting her feet and pushing the steel beam with all her strength. It groaned and shifted, then rolled free of Carol's chest.

Larissa was already at Kate's side. "We need to get her out of here."

Together, they lifted Carol—Kate supporting her shoulders, Larissa bracing her legs.

"She's burning up," Kate said, panic rising.

"Come on," Larissa urged. "To the car. Now."

Milda cleared a path through the wreckage. The warehouse lights flickered and buzzed overhead as the girls carried Carol out into the open air, hearts pounding, fear and determination driving them forward.

Eighteen

Eleanor's escape

The tires shrieked as the black sedan came skidding to a halt just outside the warehouse. Its headlights cut through the swirling dust and darkness, illuminating the cracked pavement in cold, pale beams.

Eleanor burst through the side door, her boots hitting the ground hard. Her coat flared behind her as she sprinted across the lot. The passenger door flung open before she even reached it, and she threw herself inside, slamming it shut in a single, furious motion.

A sleek gray cat, curled elegantly in the front seat, darted up onto the dashboard as Eleanor slid in, its golden eyes wide and unblinking. It moved with the fluidity of smoke, tail flicking once before it stepped gracefully onto the center console and rubbed its head against the driver's arm.

"Where's Carol?" the woman driving asked, her eyes snapping to Eleanor, though her hand paused to give the cat an absent stroke behind the ears. Her voice was tight, controlled—someone used to command.

Eleanor stared straight ahead; her jaw clenched. "Drive."

"But—"

"I said drive, Kris! Now. Head for the farm."

The car peeled away, engines growling low as it tore down the cracked industrial road and headed out of town. Behind them, the city lights grew smaller, flickering like dying stars in the rear view mirror. The buildings thinned, replaced by gas stations and closed diners. Then trees, wide fields, and the kind of creeping darkness that swallowed headlights whole.

The cat leapt softly into the backseat, its movements precise and deliberate. It settled behind Eleanor, tail coiling around its paws like a guardian shadow. Its eyes darting between the driver and the passenger.

Eleanor rested her head against the window, watching the world blur past. Her reflection in the glass looked foreign—smudged, hollow-eyed. Blood trickled down from a cut on her temple, and her hands still trembled from the strain.

Betrayal… again.

She'd been here before. Not in this car, not on this road—but in this feeling. This gut-churning, ice-cold plunge into the same wound that never healed.

First Genevieve.

Lying, simpering, pretending to be my friend while plotting behind my back. Genevieve with her soft words and gentle touch. Genevieve who had promised unity—and stolen everything. My work, my future…my husband… my legacy.

And now Carol.

Her daughter.

Her own blood.

Eleanor closed her eyes, trying to block the memory of Carol's voice— pleading, shaking, crying. *"I'm her best friend." "I can't let you kill her."*

Best friend? Eleanor's lips curled bitterly. *After everything I gave her. Raised her to be? She chose them.*

The trees thickened outside, bare branches reaching toward the car like bony fingers. The road dipped into shadow and fog.

Maybe it was her fault. She'd tried to shield Carol from the harsh truths of the world. But perhaps she'd kept her too soft. Genevieve's daughters were warriors; messy, dangerous, emotional, but still warriors.

Carol was meant to be her counterbalance. Her anchor. Her spy.

And now she was just another traitor.

Another failure.

"I should've never let her near them," Eleanor whispered to herself, voice low and cracking. "I should've done it all myself."

The cat shifted slightly behind her, letting out a soft huff, like it disagreed. Eleanor didn't turn, but her brow furrowed.

Kris said nothing.

The open fields gave way to rusted fences and the long stretch of gravel that led to the farm. The land Eleanor had hidden for years—built into a stronghold, a last sanctuary for the war she knew was coming.

As the car turned onto the dirt road, the farmhouse rose out of the darkness, its windows glowing faintly.

Eleanor straightened, drawing in a breath. There would be time for grief later—if ever. For now, there was only strategy. Recovery. Retaliation.

Carol had made her choice.

And soon, Eleanor would make hers.

Nineteen

To the hospital

Kate had one arm looped under Carol's shoulders, the other gripping her wrist as she and Larissa half-dragged, half-carried her toward the car. Milda ran ahead, yanking open the back door and clearing space. Carol's weight was heavy, limp, but still breathing, and Kate didn't let go.

Around the corner of the building, a sudden blur of motion caught their eyes. A dark grey figure on all fours came barreling toward them, paws thundering on the pavement, but clearly limping.

"Bob!" Milda shouted.

The dog skidded to a halt beside them, tail wagging in wide, frantic arcs.

"I had thought you were dead" Kate huffed. "One hit and you went down for the count."

Bob's ears flattened, and he gave a soft whine. He didn't look amused.

"I think you offended him," Larissa said, stepping aside so Kate and Milda could ease Carol into the back seat.

"Good," Kate muttered. "He is going to have to toughen up if he is going to run with the girls."

Carol groaned as they laid her down, eyelids fluttering open.

"Wait…" Her voice was gravel and air. "You were holding me…"

Kate blinked. "Yeah, to stop you from bleeding out on the floor."

"No, I mean… I felt heat." Carol's brow furrowed. "It didn't hurt as bad. It helped. Did you—?"

Kate's heart jumped. She didn't answer, not directly. Just pressed Carol's shoulder gently.

Milda slid in beside her, cradling Carol's head on her lap with surprising tenderness.

"You hate me?" Carol rasped with a weak smirk.

Milda rolled her eyes. "You're growing on me. Like…mold. Or a tragic anti-hero in a YA novel."

Carol chuckled, then winced. "Ow. Don't make me laugh. It feels like my ribs are made of cornflakes."

Bob leapt up into the back and curled beside Carol's feet, protective and alert.

Larissa got in the passenger seat, slamming the door. Kate started the car.

The city lights streaked past as they sped toward the hospital, sirens long faded and adrenaline wearing thin.

"I still can't believe it," Kate muttered. "Carol. *Carol.* The secret villain—but not. Working with Eleanor, planted in my life, and now risking everything for us."

"She saved us," Larissa said. "She saved *you.* That's not nothing."

"I'm just saying," Kate continued, "it's all a lot to process. Carol knew Eleanor this whole time. She was literally her *daughter.* That's like, a plot twist on top of a plot twist. I mean—what else don't we know? How long has she been spying on us? Does she know where the others are? Where—?"

"She's asleep," Larissa said gently.

Kate glanced back. Carol had indeed drifted off, her chest rising and falling in slow, shallow breaths. Milda had one hand resting lightly on her forehead.

Kate let out a long breath and turned her eyes back to the road.

"Okay," she said quietly. "She's asleep. We'll talk later."

They drove on in silence, the tires humming against the asphalt, the city slowly fading behind them as the weight of what had happened settled over them all.

Twenty

The farmhouse

The old farmhouse loomed ahead, shrouded in the soft blue hues of twilight. The gravel crunched under the tires as Kris slowed the car, pulling up near the front porch. A dim light glowed behind the windows, flickering like a distant memory.

Eleanor didn't wait. The moment the car stopped, she was out, her coat whipping behind her in the wind. On the porch, a man stood, a cigarette smoldering between his fingers. He watched her approach without moving.

Jack took one last drag, flicked the cigarette into the gravel, and ground it out with his boot.

"Eleanor," he greeted, voice flat.

She didn't answer. Didn't even look at him. She brushed past, boots thudding up the steps, and disappeared into the house, the screen door banging shut behind her.

Kris turned off the ignition and stepped out more slowly, stretching her back. The sleek gray cat leapt down to the ground, walking under the open door. The cat let out a small meow, watching Jack, tail raised in greeting.

Jack met Kris at the car. The cat sprang lightly onto the hood and made its way toward him. With an amused snort, Jack reached out—and the cat leapt into his arms without hesitation, purring and rubbing its face under his chin.

"Well, hey there Zara," he murmured, scratching it between the ears. "At least someone around here's glad to see me."

Kris gave a small, tired smile. "She's always liked you."

"She's got good taste," Jack said, still petting the cat. It settled against him like it had found its rightful place, content and watchful.

"Well," he muttered, nodding toward the house, "she seems chipper."

"She's a mess," Kris said, brushing windblown hair out of her face. "We found two more girls. Kate was there with two younger sisters, Milda and Larissa"

Jack tense. "And?"

"Carol turned on her," Kris said quietly, motioning at the house. "Jumped in front of something meant for one of the girls. Eleanor lost her mind. Said she's been betrayed twice now—first by Genevieve, now by her own daughter."

Jack swore under his breath. "We don't have time for this."

"No," Kris agreed. "We don't. We're supposed to be heading north, not playing out some ancient grudge match. We have three days—three—before the portal appears."

"And we're not even close to the site," Jack added. "Eleanor knows that."

"She doesn't care." Kris looked toward the house; her brow creased. "All she sees is vengeance. She keeps talking about how Genevieve 'stole everything'—how she was supposed to lead, and Genevieve took that from her. I don't know how much of it's true, but it runs deep."

Jack turned, leaning against the hood of the car, his expression tight. The cat stayed tucked in one arm, its eyes glowing faintly in the dusk. "We made a deal, Kris. We came through together. This vengeance detour was her idea—find the siblings, neutralize the threat. But the mission was always lay low for a bit and then go home."

"I know," Kris said. "But I don't think Eleanor ever planned to go back. Not if Genevieve's children were still breathing."

Jack was quiet for a long moment. Crickets sang somewhere in the fields beyond the barn. The wind rustled the tall grass, whispering secrets of worlds far beyond.

"She's going to ruin everything," he said finally.

Kris nodded. "Unless we stop her."

He glanced at her. "You willing to do that?"

She hesitated—then nodded.

"She's dangerous, Jack. And she's not thinking straight. We need to be where the convergence point is. We need to be in position, or we're stuck here for another twenty."

Jack pushed off the car, exhaling hard through his nose. "Then we better start planning. Because if we don't, we're going to be collateral damage in her war."

Behind them, inside the farmhouse, Eleanor stood at the window, watching them. Her jaw was tight. Her hands clenched at her sides.

She had not come this far to lose again. Not to Genevieve. Not to her daughter.

Not to anyone.

Twenty-One

The hospital

The car screeched to a halt in front of the emergency room entrance, as Kate threw it into park. The automatic doors whooshed open ahead, casting pale light across the pavement.

"Okay, easy—careful," Kate said, rushing to open the back door. Larissa helped slide Carol's legs out while Kate supported her upper body. Milda hovered, wide-eyed but ready, and Bob trotted around the car anxiously, tongue lolling but eyes alert.

"Okay, Carol. You with us?" Kate asked, gently nudging Carol's cheek.

Carol groaned softly, blinking at the harsh lighting above. "Did we win?"

"Let's get you inside before the victory lap," Kate muttered, her voice tight with worry.

Together, the girls maneuvered Carol out of the car, Carol's arm slung weakly over Kate's shoulder while Larissa braced her other side. Milda jogged ahead to the doors, flailing at the call button.

Bob, ever loyal, padded closely behind, tail wagging nervously. But the moment they reached the entrance, a security guard stepped into their path.

"Sorry, no dogs allowed," the man said, raising a hand as Bob tried to enter with them.

Bob growled, a deep, throaty warning that seemed to rumble through the tile beneath them. He bared his teeth and didn't back down, his eyes fixed on the guard like he was judging his soul.

"Whoa, easy, boy!" Milda said, reaching out—but Bob ignored her.

"Back up," the guard warned again, starting to reach for his radio.

"Stop." A voice cut through the tension like a blade.

Everyone turned. Dillan had come walking up the sidewalk, continuing putting himself between bob and the security guard. He stepped forward, crouched slightly, and spoke a single word in a language none of the girls recognized—guttural, melodic, and sharp all at once.

Bob immediately stopped growling.

The dog blinked once at Dillan, then gave a quiet huff and trotted outside. He settled himself in the grass near the entrance, lying down with his head up, ears twitching, watching the lot like a sentinel.

Milda gaped. "Wait a second. I *thought* you were Bob. I was *convinced* Bob was you!"

"Yeah," Kate muttered, watching Bob with narrowed eyes. "I was starting to believe it myself."

Larissa tilted her head, glancing at Dillan. "You're not completely wrong."

Dillan gave her a sly grin but said nothing.

Before Kate could question him further, a nurse rushed out with a wheelchair. "Let's get her inside!" the woman called.

The girls helped ease Carol down into the chair, Carol wincing and she let out a quiet groan. Her face was pale, drawn tight with pain.

Kate gave Milda and Larissa a pointed look. "Stay in the lobby, okay? I'll let you know what's going on as soon as I can."

"But—!" Milda began to protest, already halfway through the doors.

"No. Stay," Kate said firmly. "Please."

Milda crossed her arms and pouted. "Fine. But I'm *starving, I am going to need money for the vending machines.*"

Dillan stepped forward. "How about this—let me take you two to get something to eat and then I'll get you back to Kate's place?"

Milda's expression brightened. "Can we get macaroni and cheese?"

Dillan smiled. "I think we can make that happen."

Kate hesitated. "Okay. Thanks, Dillan."

She turned to go, then spun back. "Wait—do you know where I live?"

Dillan's expression didn't change. "I do."

Kate stared at him for a moment; lips parted.

"We're going to need to have a *very* long conversation," she said slowly.

Dillan nodded. "Soon."

Kate followed the nurse through the automatic doors, her hand still resting protectively on Carol's shoulder as they disappeared down the hallway.

Milda watched them go, then turned to Dillan. "So… what *are* you?"

Dillan smiled faintly. "Let's grab that mac n cheese first."

Twenty-Two

Farmhouse fight

The screen door creaked loudly as Kris stepped onto the front porch of the farmhouse. The air was thick with late summer warmth, crickets humming in the distance. Jack stood beside her, stroking Zara's fur, eyes scanning the horizon like he expected it to shift.

Zara leapt gracefully from his arms, landing on the porch rail before hopping down and weaving through their legs, tail high, purring like an engine.

"I'll talk to her," Kris murmured. She turned toward Jack, brushing his hair back from his brow. "We're almost there. Let's not fall apart now."

He pulled her close, their foreheads touching. Then, without hesitation, they kissed—quiet and sure, it wasn't their first time bracing for something bigger than either of them. It wasn't tender as much as resolute.

As they kissed, Zara purred louder, winding around their feet like she was blessing the moment, brushing against their calves with casual ownership.

"I'll back you," Jack said as they pulled apart. "No matter what she says."

Kris gave a single nod, squeezed his hand, then opened the door. Zara trotted ahead of them.

The farmhouse was warm, dimly lit by old lamps with amber shades.

The walls were lined with shelves of mismatched books, strange trinkets, and relics that didn't quite match this world—sharp geometric instruments, weathered parchment, a mirror that reflected too slowly. The kitchen was functional and more of this world. A copper kettle on the stove and dried herbs hanging near the window. It felt like a home lived in by necessity rather than love.

Eleanor paced the living room like a caged predator, her coat still on, boots leaving scuffs across the wood floor. Her expression was hard and unreadable, eyes burning with silent rage.

Jack moved to the high-backed armchair near the stone fireplace, sinking into it with the heaviness of someone older than he looked. As he sat, Zara immediately leapt into his lap and curled herself into a perfect spiral, her tail wrapping neatly around her body. Jack absently ran a hand down her back as he stared into the cold hearth.

Kris didn't sit. She stood in Eleanor's path and folded her arms.

"We have to talk."

Eleanor didn't stop pacing. "We don't have time for lectures."

"No, you don't have time for vendettas," Kris snapped, the exhaustion creeping into her voice. "This grudge—it's going to cost us everything. The portal, Eleanor. Our way home."

Eleanor stopped walking but didn't look at her. "So you want to run? Leave before we finish this?"

"I want to live," Kris said. "We've been here over eighty years, hiding and waiting. You promised we'd go back. That we'd find the way. And now we have it—but you're going to waste it trying to kill a dead woman's children."

"She's not dead," Eleanor growled, finally facing her. "She's out there, still breathing, still infecting this world with her weakness. Her daughters, our enemies are walking free. And you want me to forgive that?"

"It's been long enough," Kris said. "What happened back then... it was awful. I miss him too. Alexander was a great man. But he chose to protect her. Not you."

Eleanor's face twisted. "Because he was noble. Because he honored the code. Genevieve broke every law we held sacred when she married Jedrek.

She didn't just betray me, Kris. She betrayed the Realm. She threw away our legacy—for lust."

Kris flinched at the venom in her voice.

"She was reckless," Eleanor continued, voice sharp. "And because of her—because of her infatuation—the Council turned on us. We had to flee in the night like criminals, like we weren't the rightful bloodline. I was next in line. Not her. And she destroyed everything we were born to be."

Kris's voice softened. "You don't have to burn the world down to prove you were worthy."

"I *was* worthy," Eleanor snapped. "I still am."

Zara, who had been purring steadily in Jack's lap, suddenly went still. Her ears pinned back. A low hiss built in her throat, sharp and animal and utterly primal.

Eleanor turned her head sharply toward the sound.

"Zara," Kris said, her tone firm and low.

The cat stopped hissing immediately but didn't relax. Instead, she jumped from Jack's lap, her body low to the ground as she slinked across the floor and hopped onto a nearby side table. She crouched there—silent, watchful—facing Eleanor like a sentry poised for a command.

They stood like that, frozen in the storm of memory and bitterness.

Then Jack's voice cut through the silence like thunder.

"Mom!"

The word cracked through the tension, startling both women.

Eleanor turned to him, her face momentarily stricken.

Jack didn't raise his voice again. "Mom," he said, quieter. "That's enough. Kris and I have had enough. We're leaving for the portal site tonight."

Eleanor's nostrils flared. She looked between them—her son, the woman she trusted—and saw the betrayal etched on both their faces. Without a word, she stormed out the front door, the screen slamming behind her hard enough to rattle the windows.

Kris exhaled. Slowly, she walked across the room and lowered herself into Jack's lap. He wrapped an arm around her, pressing his forehead to hers.

"She'll never stop," Kris said softly.

Jack's voice was steady. "Then it's our turn. It's time we stopped hiding. It's time we ruled."

Kris leaned into him, her voice barely a whisper. "Then let's go home."

As their foreheads touched, Zara leapt lightly back into their laps, purring loud enough to drown out the crickets outside. She rubbed her face under both their chins, anointing them like she'd decided they were hers—and they were ready.

Then, as if on cue, Zara stilled. Her ears twitched. She let out a low, throaty chirp—not the contented sound from before, but something else. A call. A signal. She hopped down gracefully and padded toward the hallway, pausing only once to glance back, tail flicking with purpose.

Kris shifted. "She's right," she said softly. "It's time."

They didn't linger. Within minutes, Kris and Jack had packed what they needed, just the essentials. Old-world gear, a map etched with convergence coordinates, rations, and weapons they hoped not to use.

Kris slung her bag over her shoulder and gave the place one last glance. The air felt brittle, like the space between lightning and thunder.

Jack opened the front door. "Let's go."

Zara appeared from the shadows, slipping between their legs like smoke. She paused at the top of the porch steps.

As Jack moved forward, Zara suddenly arched her back and hissed, her fur standing on end, her eyes wide and locked on the gravel driveway ahead. She let out a sharp, guttural yowl—unnatural and jarring.

Kris threw her arm out, stopping Jack cold. "Don't move."

He froze, staring at her. "What's wrong?"

Kris didn't take her eyes off Zara. "She senses something."

And then the world split open.

The car exploded.

A deafening blast lit up the night sky in an inferno of fire and shrapnel. The shock wave knocked them backward, flames roaring where the vehicle had stood only seconds before. Heat licked across the porch like a warning.

They hit the floorboards hard. Smoke and burning rubber filled the air. Jack blinked through the haze, staring at the wreckage with disbelief. "She tried to kill us," he said, breathless. "My mother—she *knew* we were leaving."

"What do we do now?" Kris muttered, pulling herself up.

Zara let out another cry—louder, urgent—then bolted past them into the house, her tail streaming like a banner.

"Zara!" Kris called, already chasing after her. "She's heading to the back—move!"

They followed the cat, weaving through the dim living room and kitchen. Zara skidded across the hardwood and flung herself at the back door, claws scrabbling. Jack threw it open, Kris grabbed some raincoats from the hallway hook, and followed Jack out the back door.

Beyond the back porch, the tall grass swayed violently, the wind rushing in like it, too, wanted them gone.

Kris didn't look back. "The trip to the portal just got a lot harder."

Jack's jaw was tight, his eyes scanning the tree line for movement. "Then we follow her. She hasn't been wrong yet."

Zara darted down the steps and into the field, not stopping, not hesitating. They ran after her—into the night, into the wild, into the dark.

Twenty-Three

Diner, dog, & Dillan

It took three tries and one very passionate debate about the difference between *real* mac and cheese and "weird foamy garbage," but finally, they found a small diner tucked between a laundromat and a bookstore that advertised *home style cooking* on a sun-faded sign.

From the moment they walked in, the buttery scent of cheese and something fried hit them like a warm hug. Milda inhaled dramatically, as if the air alone could restore her energy.

"This," she declared, pointing to the laminated menu with reverence, "this is the place. I can *feel* it."

They slid into a booth near the window, Larissa on one side and Dillan and Milda on the other. Outside Bob sat in the grass facing the entrance. Ever alert, ears perked, he was on patrol. Milda tapped the window once and waved at him. He didn't move, but his eyes tracked them calmly.

The waitress barely had time to greet them before Milda ordered two servings of macaroni and cheese—one for her, one "for emergencies"—and a side of fries. Larissa ordered a cheeseburger, and Dillan just asked for coffee.

As soon as the waitress stepped away, Milda leaned across the table, hands flying animatedly.

"Okay, *listen.* You missed *everything.*"

Dillan raised an eyebrow. "I gathered that much."

"No. Like. You don't understand." Milda looked around to make sure no one was listening. "It was like a whole *final battle* moment. Eleanor was full-on evil. Like floaty-hands, debris-hurling evil. She tried to *crush* us, okay?"

Larissa nodded slowly. "It was intense."

"And then—and *then*—Carol *jumped in front of us*! Like, full 'nooo!' slow-mo moment. Shielded us with her whole body. Then she got totally *wrecked*. And I was like, 'Wow. She's not the villain. She's the tragic redemption arc!'"

Dillan chuckled, sipping his coffee. "So Carol switched sides."

"She didn't just switch sides," Milda said dramatically, "she did a full-on 180-character flip in the middle of the climax."

Dillan looked toward the window for a moment, his gaze falling on Bob. His eyes softened. "I'm glad she stepped in."

Milda eyed him curiously. "Yeah. Speaking of stepping in... where *were* you? And why does the dog listen to you like he's your Jedi apprentice?"

Larissa smirked. "Yeah, maybe you can fill in some of the pieces?"

Dillan leaned back, tapping a finger on his coffee cup. "Bob's not a Jedi apprentice."

"Then what is he?" Milda asked, leaning in.

Dillan hesitated, clearly weighing his words. Then he sighed. "His real name is Atlas. And he and I are bonded."

"Bonded like... best friends?" Milda asked.

"Bonded like... one soul, two bodies," Dillan said. "It's a rare ability. Some of us can form permanent links with another being. We feel what they feel. See what they see. He's a second consciousness inside my mind."

Larissa blinked. "That's... intense."

"We're bound until one of us dies," Dillan added quietly.

Milda stared. "Whoa."

Then she narrowed her eyes. "Well, I hate to tell you, but his name is now Bob. But Atlas is kind of cool too."

Outside the window, Bob—*Atlas*—suddenly stood, turned toward them, and barked once. Loudly.

Larissa jumped. "Okay, that was *weirdly* well-timed."

Milda slowly turned to Dillan, eyes wide. "Wait. Are you an alien?"

Dillan looked at her, amused. "That part of the story is for another day."

"You *totally* are," Milda whispered. "You're like… some kind of alien druid space guy."

Dillan smiled over the rim of his coffee. "Mac and cheese first. Existential crises later."

Milda shoved a fork full of Mac n Cheese in her mouth and pointed the fork at Dillan. "Okay space man, one more question."

Dillan raised one eyebrow.

"If our dad is dead, and Gwen was our sister, and we are all sisters, are we like half sisters? and where are all the dads?"

Dillan sipped slowly from his mug, clearly stalling. "I am definitely not qualified to go over the birds and bees with either of you. But I will tell you this, you are all full fledged sisters, same mom, same dad."

They finished eating as the traffic outside started to slow, the warm glow from the diner spilling onto the sidewalk. Bob remained planted by the entrance, quiet and unmoving, watching the few passing cars. Dillan paid the bill and they all loaded up.

Back at Kate's apartment, Dillan walked them up the front steps.

"You two good from here?" he asked.

"Yep," Milda said, yawning. "Full of carbs and secrets."

Dillan gave them a nod. "I'll see you soon."

As he turned to leave, Bob trotted to his side. But Dillan bent down and murmured something in that strange language again. The dog sat, tail wagging once, and stayed behind.

Larissa unlocked the door. "Is Atlas staying?"

"He's ours," Milda said proudly. "His name is *Bob*."

Bob sneezed like he agreed, then bolted between Larissa and Milda's legs and started up the stairs.

Twenty-Four

Finding their way

They didn't look back.

The farmhouse behind them stood dark and still, with an eerie glow behind it from the failed explosion. Kris led the way with a small pack slung over one shoulder, Jack close behind, his jaw tight and eyes scanning the tree line. Zara darted ahead of them in the tall grass, her grey coat nearly invisible except for the occasional flash of her eyes.

They moved quickly, sticking to the edge of the field where the moonlight couldn't quite reach. The night smelled like scorched rubber and rain-soaked soil. Smoke still drifted from the wreckage of the car, curling upward like the ghost of a plan gone wrong.

Zara paused at the edge of the field where the grass grew taller and wilder. Her ears twitched. Then, with a sudden hop, she slipped between two boulders that had once looked like part of the natural slope.

Jack frowned. "That can't be"

But Kris was already kneeling. She brushed aside a thick patch of brush, revealing a narrow, worn path just wide enough for a single person. "It's a hidden trail. An old one. I think this used to lead to the west perimeter— maybe even farther if it's still intact."

Jack looked toward the horizon, where faint hills loomed like watching giants. "That's hours on foot."

Kris stood, her face set. "We don't have a choice."

Zara turned once, waiting. Then she chirped, coaxing them forward.

They ducked into the hidden trail, the darkness wrapping around them like a cloak. Twigs snapped underfoot. The wind whispered through the canopy in a language older than memory.

Half an hour in, the path began to narrow. Roots curled like skeletal hands across the way, and the slope dipped sharply. Zara slowed, her body low to the ground, tail stiff. She let out a low growl—quiet but unmistakable.

Kris held up a hand. "Something's close."

They froze. From the shadows ahead came a rustle, then a sharp, metallic click. Out of the underbrush lumbered a shape that made the night seem colder.

It was seven feet tall, hunched, and mismatched—like it had been built out of broken pieces rather than born. One arm ended in a blade fused to bone, the other hung heavy with withered flesh stretched tight over dark, armored plating. Its face was a patchwork of human and other, with one glowing eye that twitched erratically and a mouth that opened too wide, revealing rows of rusted metal teeth. Blue energy flickered through the cracks in its chest—unstable, like a dying star trapped inside.

A remnant.

One of Eleanor's early experiments. Failed, but not forgotten.

Jack swore under his breath. "She left them out here as guards."

"Or as a warning," Kris said.

The creature hadn't moved yet. It stood in the path, watching them— breathing in short, sharp bursts, like it wasn't sure whether to charge or wait for orders that would never come.

Zara hissed again, louder this time, fur bristling like a miniature storm.

Jack raised his blade. "We take it out now. Quietly. Fast."

Kris grabbed his arm. "Wait. Look at it. It's confused. It's not defending territory, it's glitching. There's a chance we could scare it off without wasting energy or drawing attention."

He shook his head. "And if you're wrong?"

"Then we fight," she said. "But we're still hours from the convergence site. If there's more of them, we can't afford to be reckless."

They stared at the creature. It twitched again, took one step forward, then stopped.

Kris looked at Zara. "What do you think?"

As if in answer, Zara bolted from Kris's side, darting straight at the remnant. She screamed—not a cat's hiss, but something longer and stranger, a sound that cut through the night like hot wire. She arched her back and leapt at the creature's feet, clawing the ground and snarling.

The remnant stumbled back, clearly startled. Its blade-arm swung once, wide and clumsy, striking nothing. Zara darted out of reach, circling it once more before bounding off into the trees without a backward glance.

The remnant stared after her. Then, slowly, cautiously, it turned and lumbered off the trail in the opposite direction, vanishing into the dark like a shadow retreating before the dawn.

Jack blinked. "Well. I guess that solves the debate."

Kris cracked a grin. "I think her vote was for 'intimidation.'"

From the trees, Zara reappeared, trotting ahead like nothing had happened, her tail held high in quiet victory.

They followed.

The trail opened wider before them. The woods quieted again with the danger gone. Only the crunch of their boots and the occasional rustle from Zara ahead filled the space between them.

Kris adjusted the strap of her bag. "Do you think the Council still exists?"

Jack didn't answer right away. He kept his eyes on the narrow trail, jaw tight. "I don't know. If they do, they've been very quiet. We haven't heard a damn thing in twenty years."

"Maybe they fell. Maybe it all fell."

He glanced over at her. "It had already started falling before we left."

Kris nodded. "Eighty years of chaos. No crown. No center. When the royal bloodline shattered, the world did too."

"And Dad," Jack hesitated. "He died trying to get us out. He was one of the last with real authority."

"Alexander would've been a great king," Kris said softly. "And he gave that up to save us."

A long pause settled between them, heavy with memory.

"I still remember the portal flaring," she said. "That night. It was so loud, like it ripped the world in half. And then… nothing. Just this place. Dirt and steel and skies that never stopped humming."

Jack smiled faintly. "And peanut butter. Don't forget that. First thing I ever ate here."

Kris chuckled. "You were so sick."

"Worth it."

Their laughter faded.

"Do you think it's a death sentence?" Kris asked, voice low. "Going back?"

Jack's brow furrowed. "Maybe. If the Council's still in power and sees us as traitors… or if Eleanor gets there first and poisons them against us…"

"But if that message twenty years ago was true," Kris said, "then your uncle—he might still be out there. Rallying what's left."

Jack's hand tightened on the strap of his satchel. "He was in hiding. Trying to find surviving bloodlines. The guy who came through said he was calling the family home—whoever was left."

"And Eleanor killed him for it." Kris's voice turned bitter. "Right there. Didn't even ask questions. Just assumed he was the enemy."

"She didn't want Genevieve's line returning," Jack said. "Didn't want the world remembering who the true heirs were."

Kris nodded grimly. "He gave you the portal equations before she caught on. It's the only reason we even have a shot."

"I've mapped out the next two hundred years of convergence points," Jack said. "All based on that man's work. All of it… rests on whether we make it to the right place, at the right moment."

They walked a few more paces in silence.

Then Kris smirked. "Let's just hope Dillan doesn't get lost on the way."

Jack laughed. "He seemed confident."

"That's what terrifies me. My brother couldn't find his way out of a shoe box."

Jack raised a brow. "And you're trusting him to get to the portal?"

"No, I'm trusting Zara," Kris said, glancing ahead at the cat weaving through the shadows with uncanny precision. "But I *am* hoping Dillan can read your handwriting. Otherwise, we're going to have a very awkward reunion with a tree stump."

They both laughed, the sound dry and tired but real.

Ahead, Zara stopped and looked back, tail flicking once.

Kris nodded. "We're still with you, girl."

They followed her deeper into the woods, the silence folding in like a shroud.

They wouldn't make it fast. Not now.

"It's going to take three days," Jack said quietly, adjusting the weight of his pack. "Maybe more, if the terrain gets worse."

Kris glanced over her shoulder, toward the glow still flickering from the smoldering wreckage. "We can't go back to town, it's too far in the wrong direction. Too many eyes. Too many questions."

"No one we can trust," Jack agreed.

She nodded grimly. "Then it's the long way."

The trees thickened around them as they walked. Each step forward felt like a stitch pulling the past tighter around their ankles.

"But we'll make it," Kris said, more to herself than him. "We must. Dillan's counting on us."

"If he makes it on time."

Kris snorted. "Let's just hope he doesn't get lost before he convinces the girls to even show up."

Jack chuckled softly, but the weight of the days ahead pressed down again.

Zara moved ahead with certainty, silent and fluid, like she already knew the path. They followed her, each step taking them further from the lives they'd lived and closer to whatever waited on the other side of the portal.

Twenty-Five

Dillan tells all

The hospital room was dim, lit only by the soft blue glow of a monitor and the slits of sunlight seeping in through the blinds. Carol lay still beneath a thin blanket, her face peaceful but pale, a shallow bruise darkening her temple.

Kate sat in the chair beside her, legs curled up beneath her, a novel in her lap that she hadn't turned a page of in an hour. She looked up at the quiet knock on the door.

Dillan stepped in, holding two bouquets of fresh flowers. His eyes went immediately to Carol, then to Kate.

"Hey," he said softly, stepping further in. "I brought these for you and Carol. Figured you both could use something bright."

Kate smiled, stood and took the flowers. "Thanks. She'll like them. If she ever wakes up."

"She will," he said, gently. "She's tough."

Kate putting the flower on the stand next to Carol's bed and settling back into her chair. "The girls said they learned all about you last night."

"Yeah, it was easier to come clean about Atlas, uh Bob, rather than have them beat it out of me." Dillan smirked and quickly changed the subject. "How are the girls this morning, how are you?"

Kate glancing back at Carol. "Milda was weirdly calm, which honestly worries me more. Larissa was pacing like she was waiting for the lightning to strike. And I'm… I'm just trying to hold it together."

"You're doing better than most," Dillan said, settling into the chair across from her.

There was a beat of quiet.

Kate watched him closely. "If you have this connection with Bob, where were you when all of this happened?"

Dillan opened his mouth, but before he could respond, the door swung open and a doctor walked in, flipping through a chart on a clipboard.

"Good morning," he said, barely glancing up. "Carol's vitals have been stable all night. That's a good sign."

Kate stood, brushing hair from her face. "Do you have the scan results?"

"Just came in," the doctor said, tapping the chart. "Which is… well, a little unusual. You said this accident happened yesterday?"

"Right," Kate said. "Why?"

He turned the clipboard toward her, pointing at a shadow on one of the scans. "Well, according to this, she had at least two fractured ribs. But here's the thing—they've been healing for days. Maybe longer. There's early-stage calcification here and here. We'd expect some bruising, but this level of internal healing doesn't line up with a trauma from twenty-four hours ago."

Kate frowned. "But it was yesterday. I was there."

The doctor looked between them. "Then I'm not sure what to tell you. The body says otherwise. It's healing fast. Unusually fast. She's stabilizing well — almost too well, honestly. I'd like to keep her for observation another day, just to be sure we're not missing something."

He closed the chart with a snap. "She's lucky. Whatever this was, she's coming through it in record time."

With that, he gave them a polite nod and left the room.

The silence that followed was heavier than before.

Kate sat back down in the chair, looking over at Dillan again, her voice low. "You're not going to tell me what's really going on, are you?"

Dillan looked at Carol, then back at Kate. The smile he wore when he entered had faded into something steadier. He shifted in his seat, and spoke softly.

"I will," he said quietly. "Larissa said last night that Eleanor filled you in about her and Genevieve." Dillan paused, Kate nodded, and he continued.

"It would be best if I start from the beginning, a bit of a history lesson about our world."

Kate raised an eyebrow but didn't speak. Dillan leaned forward, elbows on his knees, his voice soft and steady, like he was reciting something passed down from memory.

"Our planet is called Kuiterra, it is small planet, about the size of your moon. Over two thousand years ago there was only one race of people called the Nidterans. They were a lot like humans—loved stories, built cities, made mistakes—but a few of them were different. Your word for them would be "Primes". They could heal with a touch, and bond with creatures—see through their eyes, command them if needed. They became the leaders."

Kate pointed at Dillan, he nodded and drew in a breath.

"Then, there was a crash. A ship, falling from the stars. No one really knows if it was really a crash, or if they were simply people looking for a place to escape too. On board were a few hundred people who looked just like the Nidterans… but they weren't. They had powers too; some could heal, although not as powerful as the Nidterans. But also they could see the future and some could move objects with their minds. Some of them possessed more then one power."

Dillan paused for a moment, then continued.

They called their race; Raverine. Fortunately, they were peaceful too. They were content to live apart and build their own civilization."

Kate leaned forward slightly, caught in the rhythm.

"As time went, both races started to mingle and trade. They started to build new cities together. It was a very productive era. There started to be marriage between the two races, and everything was great, they were coming together as one people. But then…" Dillan paused, looking over at Carol.

"A Prime Nidteran and a Raverine fell in love. They were both from Powerful and respected families. No one expected it to be any different then all the other multi-racial unions and life for the new couple was perfect. But, when they had children, the world changed. They had three; two boys and a girl. Born with the blood of both races, and with it, the powers of both. And when they were together, their abilities amplified."

Dillan's voice darkened.

"At first, they were seen as miraculous. But fear came quickly. The children began to enjoy their power. They pushed limits. Some say they grew cruel. People started to disappear. One story goes that the boys even killed several people just for annoying them. Eventually, the leaders from both races came to the same decision—they had to be stopped. It took years, and a lot of people died. But eventually the sister turned against her brothers, they had been manipulating her and she was horrified by what they had done. She helped to destroy them, but she died in the process. The two civilizations recovered and moved on… and a law was written: No mating between Raverine and Nidteran ever again."

His eyes moved back to Carol's sleeping form.

"Centuries passed. Peace returned. The two civilizations built a new government together, unified leadership, shared power. Certain families became royalty—symbols of balance. But then… it happened again. A royal from each race. A secret marriage, and it was hinted that they were expecting a child. When it was discovered, panic spread like wildfire. The old fear came back stronger than ever."

Kate's voice was soft. "What happened to them?"

"They ran," Dillan said. "They used a technology close to what you would call a portal. They disappeared, but not just them, their entire families for fear of being executed."

His gaze turned sharp, locked on her.

"Some came here. Your Mom, Eleanor, Me and some close friends. Eleanor had the most to lose, she was next in line to rule Kuiterra, she is the equivalent of a princess…But Eleanor loved Genevieve. It was a big decision for Eleanor and her husband, Alexander, who if you remember was Genevieve's brother, so your uncle."

Kate looked at Dillan, stunned.

"And you?"

Dillan gave a slow, solemn nod. "As you guessed, I'm Prime Nidteran. My family line has always been charged with protecting the princesses… wherever they are. That is how my brother and your mother met…"

He leaned back, voice heavy with truth.

"Twenty years ago, a man came looking for members of the royal family. He carried information—equations, coordinates. He told us Eleanor's Uncle was still alive, rallying allies. Calling the royal family's home. That's why he came. Eleanor killed him before he could finish what he started. She didn't want any of you to return."

He leaned closer, his tone was no longer a storyteller's, but a soldier's.

"You and your sisters, Kate… you're the children of that forbidden union. Because of your mother and father, our world has been torn apart. You have the potential to destroy our civilization or possibly bring it back together."

Kate didn't speak. She couldn't.

The words hung in the air like dust after an explosion—too dense to breathe, too unreal to ignore. Descendants of a forbidden union. Blood that had changed a world. A past that had chased them across galaxies.

She sat back slowly, her gaze drifting to the sleeping form of Carol. Her friend. Her enemy. Her… cousins in something ancient and terrifying. She opened her mouth, then closed it again. Her brain was still trying to catch up with her heart.

Carol stirred.

It was just a twitch at first, then a groggy shift beneath the hospital sheets. Her eyes fluttered open, unfocused at first, until they found Kate's face. She blinked.

"Kate?" Carol asked confused.

Kate straightened, voice soft but steady. "Hey."

Carol looked around the room, then back to Kate. "What happened?"

"You passed out," Dillan said gently, stepping closer. "They've been running scans all night. You're healing faster than normal."

Carol's brows wrinkled. She started to sit up, wincing slightly.

"How do you feel?" Kate asked, voice unsure. There was a strange, heavy distance in the space between them—like one was floating and the other was sinking.

"Like I got hit by a truck and the truck apologized and tried to hug me after," Carol muttered, then glanced between the two. "What... did I miss?"

Dillan gave a small smile. "Just a little history lesson."

Carol's gaze flicked toward Kate again—something unreadable in her eyes. Dillan cleared his throat.

"I should go get you something better than gelatin and pudding. Maybe something warm," he said, already moving toward the door. "Kate, you good here?"

She nodded, though her throat felt tight. "Yeah. I'm good."

Dillan paused at the door, then stepped out.

Silence settled between the girls.

Carol fidgeted with the edge of the blanket. She wouldn't meet Kate's eyes. "I didn't know, not at first. And when I did... I didn't know how to stop it. Didn't know what to say. I didn't even know who I was, and then I found out I was" Her voice caught. "I thought I had to choose. Her or you."

Kate was quiet, absorbing every word. The tension in her chest was cracking now, not from anger, but something sadder. Deeper.

"And now?"

Carol looked up at her, eyes rimmed with guilt. "Now I know she never gave me a real choice."

Kate's lip trembled, just for a moment. "You lied to me, our time together was a lie. You let her use you. You let her hurt people I care about."

"I know, but our time together was real, you have become my sister" Carol said quickly, voice breaking. "I hate myself for it. I tried to make it right. I don't expect you to forgive me."

Kate shook her head slowly. "That's the thing. I don't know if I can... but I don't want to lose you either."

Carol held her gaze at Kate with raw intensity, "You don't have to trust me right now. I just want the opportunity to earn it back. I want to be someone you can trust."

There was a long pause. Kate took Carol's hand and squeezed it.

"I cannot believe how strange my life has become, how strange our lives have become," Kate said, giving a tiny, broken laugh. "I am not sure how to make it through another day of all this."

Carol swallowed hard, a tear slipping down her cheek. "Together."

The girls sat in silence, their hands still clasped. Not everything was forgiven. But some had begun to heal.

The silence hung, not as heavy, just fragile, like the moment might break if either of them breathed too loudly.

Kate shifted in her seat, finally letting out a slow exhale. "So…" she said, her tone light but still shaky, "you're a princess. Like… tiara and everything?"

Carol groaned, burying her face in her hands. "Ugh."

Kate grinned weakly. "Your Highness."

Carol rolled her eyes but smiled anyway. "If I'm a princess, that makes you one too. We're cousins, remember?"

Kate's face froze, then dropped into mock horror.

"Yep." Carol paused for a minute, dropping her smile. "It was so hard all these years, I wanted to share everything with you. I am so sorry." Carol dropped her head staring at the end of the bed.

"Hey, we are here now sharing. It is going to take time."

Kate smiled, the warmth between them cautiously growing again. Both of them sat silent, new hope for their future.

The buzz of Dillan's phone on the rolling table broke the silence, instinctively Kate looked over at it. It was a text message from Jack, Kate read it out loud.

"Kris and I are on the run, Eleanor is out of control, meet you at the portal." Kate looked at Carol. "Do you want to tell me about the portal? Or shall I wait for Dillan."

Carol looked worried, but then smiled, "Let's wait for Dillan, it will be more fun that way."

Kate's brow furrowed slightly, her voice dipping back into something quieter. "Do you know what Dillan is?"

Carol's smile faded. She nodded slowly. "Yeah. I do."

"And?"

Carol hesitated. "I lied before. I said I didn't know him. But I've known Dillan since I was a kid. He was… he was supposed to protect my mother."

Kate blinked. "Seriously?"

"He was her sworn guard. Like, oath-bound or something. But—he wouldn't do everything she asked. Especially once she started getting… darker."

"Darker how?"

"She wanted him to kill. Eliminate people who got in her way. He refused. So, she turned on him. Tried to have him killed."

Kate sucked in a breath. "Damn."

"He barely got away," Carol continued, eyes distant. "But instead of running, he decided to find the rest of you. Genevieve's children. The ones she was hiding."

Kate was quiet, letting the pieces settle in her mind.

"He's been in contact with me over the years," Carol admitted. "Trying to help me see who she really is. I didn't want to believe him. At first, I thought he was just bitter, or trying to turn me against her."

"And now?"

Carol looked at her, eyes heavy. "Now I know he was right. I knew for a long time. But it's hard, you know? She's, my mom. She raised me, lied to me, trained me, kept me close like I was some kind of… weapon. But she also held me when I was sick. Told me stories. Made me feel like I mattered."

She shook her head slowly. "I didn't know how to stop following her. Until I met you. Until I started feeling like I was betraying *you* every time I didn't speak up."

Kate's throat tightened again, and she gave Carol's hand another small squeeze. "You're not a weapon, Carol."

Carol smiled, watery and soft. "Neither are you."

There was another beat of silence between them, filled only by the quiet hospital hum and the low murmur of voices outside the door.

Kate wiped her eyes. "Well, this is officially the weirdest family reunion

I've ever had."

Carol laughed. "Welcome to the royal bloodline."

A soft knock tapped on the hospital room door before it opened again. Dillan stepped in, holding a small paper bag in one hand and a drink in the other.

"I come bearing gifts," he said, lifting the items slightly. "The vending machine was a wasteland, but the cafe had real food. Sort of."

Carol blinked quickly and gave a small, sheepish smile. "You didn't have to…"

"Yeah, well," Dillan said, setting the items on the rolling table beside her bed, "don't thank me yet, you haven't tried it."

He glanced between the two girls, his expression softening. "You two okay?"

Kate nodded. "We're… figuring it out."

"Good," Dillan said with a slight nod folding his arms. "You should eat. You'll need your strength."

Carol pulled the table closer and started opening the bag.

Kate had many more questions. "So… who are Kris and Jack?"

Dillan looks up, blinking. His arms unfold slowly. "How do you know about them?"

Kate shrugged, "your phone went off while you were out."

Carol shifts slightly in bed. She winces a little but lifts her head. "They were with us."

Carol stopped and looked into Kate's eyes realizing she had absently looped herself back in with her mother. "…with Eleanor. They came through the portal."

Dillan walks over and lowers himself into the other chair, sitting fully back.

"They're not like Eleanor. Not really. But they followed her for a long time. Jack especially."

Kate was finally getting some answers and was not stopping, "Why?"

"Because Jack is her son." Dillan said quietly.

Kate's eyes widened. She glances at Carol, "Your brother?" Carol nodded faintly.

Dillan continued, "Eleanor has always used people… twisted their loyalty. That your family were a threat. That you and your sisters were dangerous, born of something that shouldn't exist."

As Dillan paused, Carol added, "She fed him lies, she fed all of us lies. And Kris… she just stayed because of Jack. Which is ironic, because Kris is Prime Nidteran." Carol chuckled and shook her head.

Kate scrunched her face. "Wait isn't that illegal? Isn't that the whole reason for all this….Shit show?"

Dillan leans forward, elbows on his knees again.

"I've been trying to get through to them. I think Kris has been done for a while and I think maybe she is bringing Jack around as well. They have always just wanted to go home."

Kate motioned to Dillan's phone "Well from the text you got, they are done and will meet you at the Portal?"

Dillan absent mindedly picked up his phone reading the text. "Well, that is good news."

"So… can we trust them?" Kate glanced down at the phone again.

Dillan didn't answer immediately. He sat his phone down on the table and looked out the window. "A minute ago, I would have said, not yet. But with this message, yeah, we have two more allies."

The silence returns, but it's heavier now. Full of thoughts unspoken.

Carol closes her eyes briefly, then speaks just above a whisper.

"Well there is only one way to find out for certain."

Kate looks at them both. "The portal."

A faint knock at the door, and Dillan rose quickly, almost as if he was glad to not start the next conversation. Dillan had barely cracked the door open when it was nearly flung back in his face.

"Larissa—!" he started, stepping back.

Larissa swept into the room like a storm, with Milda on her heels and John trailing behind them looking apologetic.

"Carol!" Larissa said, her voice was too loud for a hospital. "Are you okay?

You look… well, not dead, so that's something."

Before Carol could answer, Milda had zeroed in on the tray next to her bed.

"Ooh. Is that real food?" she said, already snatching the sandwich with both hands. "Mmmf. Yep. Real enough."

Dillan blinked, stepped fully aside, and gave John a nod. The two men shook hands briefly, a quiet exchange in the middle of the chaos.

Kate narrowed her eyes. "Wait—how do *you* know Dillan?"

John glanced her way, casually sticking his hands in his jacket pockets. "Met him last night. He dropped off the girls. I caught him just before he walked away and invited him up for coffee."

"You *met* him?" Kate's tone edged toward suspicions.

John lifted an eyebrow, then gave her a lopsided smile. "Yeah. We had quite a conversation. Nice guy. Thought you might like him." He gave her a look—pointed, teasing, and absolutely impossible to misinterpret.

Kate blushed despite herself. "That's not—"

"He told your dad everything," Milda said through a mouthful of food, crumbs flying. "Like, *everything everything*." She waved half a sandwich in the air and turned to Carol. "Did you know we're actually *princesses?*"

Carol blinked. "Uh—"

"I need a tiara. And like, a royal decree or something. Can we knight people? What's the budget for a royal wardrobe?" Milda rambled on, now pacing like she was in a press conference.

Larissa slumped into Dillan's empty chair beside the bed, smirking at the chaos. "This is what I've been dealing with."

But Carol's attention had snapped toward John. Her expression fell as the weight of Milda's words sank in.

"Wait," she said slowly. "When she said *everything*… does that mean you know about…"

John met her gaze, reading the hesitation. "Yeah," he said simply. "Dillan told me. About your mom. About you."

Carol swallowed, eyes dropping to her lap. "I'm sorry. I didn't want to hurt", carol caught her breath, "either of you."

John shrugged, his voice easy. "Family pressure's a real thing. And your mom—well, sounds like she's got a whole planet's worth of baggage."

Carol let out a small, grateful breath. "Still, thank you."

John gave her a half-smile.

"No more deep emotional conversations" Larissa added trying to lighten the conversation. "My brain cannot take it anymore."

Milda, now balancing Carol's dessert pudding in one hand and her spoon in the other, said, "Do I get royal powers too, or is that only for firstborns?"

Larissa muttered, "God help us if it's birth order."

Kate shot Larissa a sideways glance, finally catching on that Larissa's dig was meant for her.

Larissa grinned.

Dillan, who'd been standing quietly by the door this whole time, glanced at the tray Milda had just about cleaned out. "I'll go grab you something else, Carol. I should've known it wouldn't survive."

"I'll go," John offered, already stepping toward the door.

"I'm coming too," Milda said, hopping up and licking pudding off her thumb. "I'm still starving. Hospital portions are not big enough."

Larissa rolled her eyes but stood as well. "Fine, I'll come. Someone has to supervise."

As she reached the door, she paused and looked back. "Hey, before we go… has anyone filled Kate in on the portal yet?"

Kate blinked. "You know about the portal, everyone knows about the portal except me"

Larissa just grinned. "Cool. Have fun with that," she said, slipping out with the others.

The door had barely clicked shut behind Larissa before Kate turned on Dillan and Carol, her arms crossed and her jaw tight.

"Okay. Someone please start explaining the portal."

Dillan straightened from the wall, his tone calm but serious. "The portal is a passageway. A doorway between Earth and our home world—Kuiterra. There are others, too. Portals that link to different places, different worlds.

But they're rare, and their timing is, precise. Calculated down to the second. Different location, different conditions, and many years apart."

He let that settle before continuing. "The last one between Earth was over twenty years ago. There hasn't been one since, until now."

Kate frowned. "So what happened back then?"

Dillan glanced at Carol, then continued. "A man came through. He was sent by your grandfather, Eleanor's Uncle."

"Wait," Kate said, holding up a hand. "Back up. Grandfather?"

"Your mother's dad," Dillan clarified. "He was one of the few who survived when the royal families were overthrown. He had decided to stay behind. The man who came through the portal carried his message, specifically meant for your mother, but also for Eleanor. They had no idea what had happened here between your mom and Eleanor. He brought coordinates, equations—a map of portal activity for the next two hundred years. He was here to find your mother. To bring her back."

Kate blinked, stunned. "What happened to him?"

Dillan's voice lowered. "He found Eleanor first. Eleanor killed him. She figured out why he was here and what he meant to do. He never reached your mother. The only reason any of us know this is because of Jack and Kris. They were with Eleanor when the man showed up."

Kate stood silent for a moment, absorbing the weight of it all. Then a realization hit her, sharp and cold. Her eyes narrowed as she looked at Dillan. "Wait… if the last portal was twenty years ago… and you didn't come through that one…"

Her gaze flicked to Carol. "How long have you two been here?"

Neither of them answered immediately. Dillan's expression stayed even.

Carol shifted uncomfortably, looking very apologetic. "I was born here; but I am a bit older than you. I'm twenty-six"

Kate's mouth dropped as she processed more of the lie.

Kate's voice grew more incredulous, turning towards Dillan. "Exactly how long have you *been* here? How old are you?"

Dillan met her gaze. "Old enough to remember what our world looked like before it fell apart. We have been blending in for a long time. Changed names. Changed everything."

Kate stared, speechless.

Then she shook her head slightly, voice suddenly sharp again. "So the portal, it is the way back to your planet. It's opening soon?"

Dillan hesitated.

Kate's voice sharpened more. "How long until it opens?"

Carol spoke softly. "Two days."

Kate turned to her. "You knew?"

Carol nodded, guilt heavy in her eyes. "Yes."

"You *knew*, and you didn't tell me?" Kate's voice cracked with disbelief. "You let me sit here, thinking I had time. That this was just… some weird history lesson?"

"I wanted to," Carol said. "I didn't know how, everything's been happening so fast. You were hurt and I—"

"I have two days?" Kate asked, stepping back, voice barely above a whisper.

"Two days to decide," Dillan said. "Kris and Jack are already on their way. The portal is only open for about three minutes. If you miss it… the next one won't be for another twenty years."

Carol added gently, "They're expecting us. All of us."

Kate stared at them both, her pulse pounding in her ears.

"Right," she muttered. "No pressure."

Kate needed air. Space. Something that wasn't this tiny room packed with impossible truths.

Without a word, she turned and walked to the door. Her hand paused on the handle.

"I just need…" she started, but didn't finish. She didn't know what she needed.

Dillan took a small step toward her. "Kate—"

"I'm not running off," she said, her voice steadier than she felt. "I'm just… checking on the girls. And my dad. I need to breathe for a second."

Carol nodded silently, her face still pale but understanding.

Kate stepped into the hallway. The sterile hospital scent hit her like a wave—sharper now, somehow grounding.

"Hey," Dillan's voice from behind. "You, okay?". He closed the door and stepped completely into the hallway as Kate turned to meet him.

Kate nodded, then shook her head. "It's just… a lot. Everything you've told me, everything I've seen—it's hard to wrap my head around."

Dillan took a step closer. "I know. That's why I came out, I wanted to make sure you know I am here for you. Not just for a history lesson, not as some protector, but for you."

He reached up and gently brushed a strand of hair from her face, his fingers trailing lightly along her cheek before sliding behind her ear and curling around the back of her neck. He paused there, eyes searching hers for any sign to stop.

Kate leaned in, slowly, heart thudding in her chest.

That was all the answer Dillan needed. He closed the space between them, drawing her in as his lips met hers, tender at first, then just a bit deeper with a quiet intensity.

When they finally pulled apart, Kate's eyes fluttered open. She smiled, a little breathless.

"That helped," she said.

Dillan laughed. "Good. I was hoping it might. Go get some air." With that Dillan turned and headed back in with Carol. Kate stood there for a moment watching him disappear. She turned and headed back down the hallway.

Neither of them noticed the figure down the hall, half-shadowed near the vending machines, standing perfectly still.

Eleanor's eyes followed Kate as she walked past, the corners of her mouth tight with something unreadable—rage, disappointment, calculation. Maybe all three. She stood silent in the fluorescent lights and dull tile space, blending into the scene of people waiting and worrying.

Eleanor's gaze turned back on the door Dillan had just entered. So close.

Then without hesitation she turned, disappearing down another hallway, as silent and surgical as a blade sliding into flesh.

Kate kept walking, unaware, her thoughts miles away. She instinctively followed the exit signs and headed out into the hospital's courtyard.

The black bird with the purple ring around it's neck swooped down in front of her squawking twice and then disappearing into the trees.

"Exactly what are you trying to tell me?" Kate yelled at the trees but no answer came.

She wandered on.

Bob found her, fell into step at her side, silent but looking up at her. "I am fine Bob, uh Atlas". Bob gave her a slight nudge, and they continued to walk. Kate had to smile as they passed a swing hanging from a tree. The nightmares: how horrific those dreams had seemed, and now after everything else, it seemed childish to have been so shaken by them.

After what felt like an eternity of swirling thoughts and emotions, Kate decided she should indeed check in on her dad and the girls. She said a quick goodbye to Bob, who settled back into the grass at the entrance.

Following the signs toward the cafeteria, Kate was unsure what she would even say when she got there. She wasn't even sure she could speak.

She just needed to see her dad… and Milda, Larissa. The people she knew. The people she could trust.

She just needed something to feel normal again, but she couldn't even remember what that was.

Twenty-Six

Eleanor Confronts Mary

The wind cut through the trees, pushing the rain sideways, scattering brittle leaves across the pavement as Eleanor strode purposefully toward the orphanage. The heels of her boots clicked with sharp finality against the sidewalk, each step steady, deliberate, almost too quiet for how much rage simmered just beneath her skin.

The old building loomed ahead, squat and weather worn, with vines creeping up its brick sides like veins feeding a long-forgotten heart. It had once been a sanctuary—for children, for the broken, for the lost. Eleanor had found comfort here once too, in the early days, back when she and Mary had been on the same side.

Back before everything went wrong.

Her fingers twitched at her side, brushing the fabric of her tailored coat. She could still picture the old days: Mary bustling through the halls with her endless energy, her naive belief in rules and fairness. Catherine tagging behind her, so eager to prove herself. And Eleanor—quiet, watchful, already knowing the world was never going to be kind to any of them.

But Mary had changed. Grown weak. Sentimental.

Eleanor sneered as she pushed open the wrought-iron gate. It creaked in protest—an old, familiar sound—and she didn't bother to shut it behind her.

Let the wind do that. Let the wind clean up what was left.

She climbed the stairs, her gloved hand brushing the wooden banister. Faded paint chipped beneath her touch. A child's drawing fluttered from a bulletin board in the entryway—crayon hearts and stars surrounding the word *family*.

Eleanor paused, her jaw tightening.

Foolish sentiment. None of it lasts.

She moved down the hallway, rain dripping to the floor. Her boots muffled now by a runner rug frayed from years of small feet racing to breakfast. The scent of apple cinnamon oatmeal and cleaning supplies lingered faintly in the air. It struck her with an unexpected pang. Memory. Muscle-deep.

She pushed it down.

At the end of the hall, she stopped before Mary's office and knocked once—sharp and unnecessary—before turning the handle.

The office door creaked open.

Mary looked up from her desk, her pen frozen mid-signature. Across from her, Catherine slowly stood from the visitor chair, eyes narrowing as Eleanor stepped into the room like she owned it. Her heels clicked deliberately against the linoleum floor, every movement a performance.

"Eleanor," Mary said coolly, her voice brittle.

Eleanor shut the door behind her with an almost lazy push, then turned the lock. "Hello, Mary." She smiled, but it didn't reach her eyes. "I thought I might drop by. It's been… what? A few years?"

Eleanor turned her gaze to Catherine. "Catherine? your still alive?"

Catherine stepped in front of Mary. "You're not welcome here."

"Oh, I never was," Eleanor purred. She drifted over to the bookcase, ran her fingers along the dusty spines of social work manuals, and plucked one at random. With a careless toss over her shoulder, it slammed into the wall behind Mary's head. "Oops."

Mary didn't flinch. "What do you want?"

Eleanor picked up a framed photo of the orphanage's first graduating class. "I came for a chat. A reunion. Maybe a reckoning."

She let the photo fall from her hand. It shattered on the floor.

"You've been whispering things, Mary," Eleanor said, pacing slowly. "Poisoning young minds. Encouraging disobedience. Treason really. You've gotten quite bold in your old age."

"I told the truth," Mary said, her voice trembling but clear.

Eleanor turned sharply. "The truth?" She laughed, loud and sharp. "You wouldn't know the truth if it strangled you. At least you didn't tell them about the portal."

Mary took the bait, "Portal, what portal?"

"Opps, did I say portal, well you won't be alive long enough to share that little secret." With a flick of her wrist, she sent a glass paperweight flying toward Catherine. It shattered on the door frame, shards skittering across the tile.

Eleanor's fingers twitched again, and the glass frame of a nearby photo cracked with a sharp *snap*.

"I should burn this place to the ground."

"And what would that solve?" Mary snapped. "You're chasing ghosts, Eleanor. All you're doing is proving you've already lost."

For a second, something flickered behind Eleanor's eyes. Not pain. Not doubt. Something colder. A deep, calcified disappointment.

"You always were weak," she whispered.

And then, with a flick of her wrist, a heavy vase lifted from a nearby table and hurled itself straight at Mary.

Twenty-Seven

The Cafeteria

The cafeteria buzzed with low conversation and the clatter of trays. The scent of pizza, overly buttered rolls, and something suspiciously resembling broccoli soup hung in the air.

Kate pushed open the door and slipped inside, her face pale and drawn. She scanned the room and spotted Larissa, Milda, and John near the back, clustered around a rectangular table piled high with half-finished trays and condiment packets. Milda was enthusiastically sampling something from every plate, humming with satisfaction as she chomped on a fry from John's tray.

John looked up first. He stood halfway, brow furrowing as Kate approached. "You okay?" he asked quietly.

Kate gave a small shake of her head, brushing it off. "I just needed a break. Some air."

She slid into the seat beside Larissa. Milda, noticing her for the first time, paused mid-bite with a mouthful of tater tots. She blinked at Kate's expression, then reached across the table and slid her untouched bowl of macaroni and cheese over.

"Here," she said through a full mouth. "You look like you need this more than me."

Kate huffed a soft, surprised laugh. "Thanks."

John sat back down. He glanced at her, "So… they told you about the portal."

Kate didn't answer at first. Her eyes lifted slowly. "You knew?"

John nodded. "Dillan told me last night."

Kate leaned back, a wave of relief crossing her face. "Good. At least I don't have to explain it to you."

From across the table, Milda blinked. "Wait—what's a portal?"

Larissa gave her a look and quietly shushed her.

Kate pressed a palm to her forehead. "What am I going to do?"

John reached out, placing a reassuring hand on hers. "Whatever you decide—"

Before he could finish, Larissa's fork clattered to the floor.

Her eyes glazed over.

She sat bolt upright, fingers tightening against the edge of the table. Her breath hitched sharply.

"Lari?" Kate leaned forward, concern replacing the heaviness in her voice. "Larissa, are you okay?"

But Larissa didn't respond. Her eyes were locked on something far away, something none of them could see.

As Kate reached to touch her shoulder, Milda, completely oblivious, reached over and snuck a chicken tender from Larissa's plate, nibbling silently as she stared at her sister.

Then Larissa blinked—once, twice—and gasped as though surfacing from water.

"She's in trouble," she said, breathless.

John sat forward. "Who?"

"Mary." Larissa's voice shook. "She's in her office. Eleanor is there. She's—she's hurting her."

Kate pushed her chair back instantly, already on her feet. "We have to go. Now."

Twenty-Eight

Eleanor's Confrontation

"Enough of this," Mary snapped. "You want to lecture? Fine. But leave those girls alone, do not hurt them!"

"Always so noble," Eleanor said, almost fondly. She perched on the corner of Mary's desk like she belonged there.

"Do you remember Gwen?"

Mary stiffened.

Eleanor continued before Mary could speak. "because, I do," her voice lower now. "I remember how she begged you to help her. How you told her to walk away. Told her it wasn't her fight."

Mary's hands clenched the edge of her desk.

"She wanted to protect those girls," Eleanor said, eyes gleaming. "And look where it got her. She died because of it."

"That is a lie," Mary hissed, standing. "You're the reason Gwen died! She was trying to protect them from *you!*"

The air grew thick with tension.

Eleanor's smile vanished.

"Careful," she said, voice like ice. "You forget who you're speaking to."

Mary opened her mouth to respond—but too late.

With a sharp flick, Eleanor sent the letter opener on Mary's desk flying, a silver streak aimed straight for her chest.

"NO!" Catherine lunged.

The blade caught her in the side as she knocked Mary back. The two of them crashed to the floor, Mary catching Catherine in her arms as they both fell into a heap.

"Catherine!" Mary cried, her voice cracking.

Catherine groaned, blood spreading quickly through her blouse.

Eleanor stood, silent for a moment, breathing harder than before. Then, distant shouting echoed from the front hallway—footsteps thundering.

Eleanor's head jerked up.

She turned toward the side exit and muttered, "This isn't over."

Then, like a shadow melting away, she was gone.

Twenty-Nine

Orphanage Rescue

By the time they reached the orphanage, Larissa had already had John call ahead.

"Two women," he repeated breathlessly to the operator. "Wounded. Possibly critical. Send an ambulance to the orphanage. Now."

John stayed on the line, running behind them as the girls burst through the entrance, Bob leading the way.

Kate's heart pounded in her throat. She sprinted down the main hallway behind Bob, Larissa and Milda at her heels, John's voice trailing behind them as he relayed directions to the dispatcher.

Bob took a sharp left down a side hallway before Mary's office, his back fee sliding out from under him as he took the corner. Barking loudly like a command. Kate knew exactly what he said. He was going after Eleanor; Kate was to take care of Mary and Catherine. As she ran past the hallway she could see Bob, leaping out the exit door at the end of the hallway, she turned her attention back to her destination, the door at the end.

The door to Mary's office was ajar, splinters clinging to the broken lock. Kate shoved it open and froze.

Mary sat on the floor, slumped against the wall, her blouse torn and soaked in blood. In her arms, Catherine lay limp and pale, her face peaceful despite the small crimson wound in her side.

"No—no, no, no," Kate whispered, rushing to their side. "Mary!"

Mary's head rolled toward her. She was conscious but fading fast, her face twisted with pain and grief. She didn't react to the sound of Milda gasping behind her or Larissa falling to her knees beside Catherine.

"She didn't deserve this," Mary rasped, her voice raw. "She was just trying to protect me."

"I know," Kate whispered, reaching for her hand. "Help is on the way."

Mary coughed, her hand trembling as she gripped Kate's. "It's not over. Eleanor won't stop. She never does."

"We'll fight her," Larissa said, tears running down her cheeks.

"You can't stay here," Mary said, forcing the words past her pain. "You have to go through the portal."

Kate's eyes widened. "Mary—"

"She'll kill you all," Mary said. "She's too far gone. You need to go home. Your real home."

Behind them, heavy boots echoed in the hallway.

John appeared, leading two paramedics in full gear. He moved aside so they could get to Mary and Catherine, his face pale and drawn.

"She's gone," Larissa said quietly, still holding Catherine's hand.

One of the medics nodded grimly and gently began to separate Catherine from Mary's grasp while the other moved to assess Mary's injuries. Mary cried out weakly as they lifted her, and the girls stepped back to give them space.

"She's been stabbed," the medic confirmed. "We've got her. Let's get her to County General now."

Kate stood, her limbs trembling, mind reeling.

Mary's voice echoed in her ears.

Go through the portal.

Larissa stepped beside her, face pale but calm. "We need to decide. Soon."

John turned, locking eyes with Kate, his voice quiet. "She isn't going to stop, is she?"

Kate didn't answer. She couldn't.

All she could do was stare at the bloodstained floor where Catherine had fallen—and realize that Mary was right.

If they stayed, Eleanor would destroy everything.

The paramedics carefully lifted Mary onto the stretcher. Her face was pale, lips cracked, but her eyes fluttered open again as they wheeled her toward the door.

She reached out weakly, fingers brushing against Kate's arm.

"There's… something else," she whispered. "Gwen's journal. I found it. It's… in my desk. Bottom drawer."

Kate's breath caught. "Gwen's Journal?"

Mary nodded. "Answers… memories… maybe something… to help you." Her eyes drifted closed again, her grip loosening.

The medic at her side called out her vitals as they wheeled her quickly down the hallway.

The girls stood there for a long moment in silence. The office felt cavernous now, empty even with all of them inside it. The quiet buzz of the fluorescent lights was the only sound left behind.

Larissa moved first, stepping behind Mary's desk and opening the bottom drawer. She pulled out a worn leather journal, wrapped in a faded blue ribbon. The initials "G.W." were engraved softly into the cover.

"This is it," she said, her voice hushed with reverence.

Kate reached for it, holding it to her chest like it might fall apart if she wasn't careful. "Let's go home."

Milda sniffled but nodded, sticking close to Kate as they walked out of the office together. Bob padded up quietly behind them, his tail stiff and his ears twitching. Although his chase was over he could still sense danger in the air.

John fell into step, his hand resting gently on Larissa's shoulder.

They said nothing else as they stepped out into the night, the ambulance pulling away into the distance with Mary inside, sirens off but lights still flashing.

It had been a long day—too long. And somehow, they all knew it wasn't over yet.

But for now… they needed rest. Time to breathe. Time to read.

Time to figure out what came next.

Thirty

Gwen's Journal

The neighborhood was quiet, the rain had stopped, leaving puddles that only added to the dreary emotions of the night. After everything that had happened, the girls stumbled into the apartment, utterly drained. They had barely spoken, just enough to agree on ordering pizza. Each had taken long showers, trying to scrub away the fear, the blood, and the weight of everything they had seen.

They had agreed to save Gwen's journal until morning.

John, always the early riser, had already made a full breakfast by the time they emerged from their bedrooms. The scent of bacon and cinnamon had crept down the hall, dragging Milda out first. She had devoured her share of pancakes and eggs, but it was the cinnamon rolls that had stolen her heart. He had made them from scratch, and the last one now sat on her plate, her fork poised for the final battle.

Larissa was at the sink finishing the dishes, sleeves pushed up and hair tied back, methodically scrubbing the last plate. Kate had helped clean up too, but she was already curled on the couch, journal in hand.

John sat at his desk nearby, tapping away on his laptop and frowning over a stack of unpaid bills.

"You ready?" Kate asked, nodding at the journal.

Milda, her mouth full, mumbled, "Yes."

They settled onto the couch, Milda squishing herself into the middle spot, the journal now resting in her lap. Kate to her left, Larissa to her right. The moment felt heavy. Like opening the journal would open more than memories. It would open truths.

The first entries were simple—childish handwriting describing life at the orphanage. Gwen had drawn the playground in surprising detail, her new friends, the nuns, the quiet hours in the study. Her sketches were astonishing: detailed portraits of girls long gone, scenes from recess, even a picture of Mary pouring orange juice.

But the journal shifted a few pages in.

The entries became dreamlike. Gwen began recording her visions. One after another. Drawings came with them, precise and haunting.

There was a picture of the two women from the photograph—the woman with the cold eyes locking the other in a steel room aboard a zeppelin. Another drawing showed the same ship engulfed in flames, mid-air.

Kate flipped to a page dated just days before Gwen's death. Gwen described how every day she dreaded stepping outside, waiting to see if it matched what she had seen in her visions. She had seen her own death so many times, she wrote, she barely felt fear anymore. Only exhaustion.

The drawing accompanying it was simple. Two small hands, palms up, in the foreground. In the distance, Mary walked slowly toward her.

Larissa pressed her hand to her mouth. Her eyes shimmered. "She knew. Every single day she waited for it to happen."

Kate slid her arm around Larissa's shoulder, pulling her in. The three girls sat in silence, sharing Gwen's sorrow.

Then Milda turned the page.

They all gasped.

It was them.

The drawing showed the three of them exactly as they were now. Sitting on the couch. Milda in the middle. Larissa crying softly. Kate comforting them both.

"Holy crap," Milda whispered.

Kate began reading the message beneath it out loud.

"Hello Sisters. I am sorry I will not get to meet you, I would have liked to be there with you, but I have seen you so many times in my dreams that I feel like I am. I do not want to share too much, as you know Larissa, sharing your visions is just as dangerous as trying to change the outcome. But I wanted to tell you that not everything will be as it seems. Your friends may be your enemies, or they may just seem to be your enemies. Let the journey play out in front of you, but always, always rely on each other. You are sisters. Tell our mother that I loved her, and we danced often in my dreams.

Gwen."

None of them spoke for a while.

Finally, Larissa sniffed and wiped her face with her sleeve. "There's more," she said.

Kate groaned, rubbing her temple. "I'm not sure I can take another."

Milda carefully turned the page.

The drawing was different from the others. Strange and open. It was a meadow, wide and sunlit. A dense forest loomed at the edge, and in the center was a thick tree stump. Wide enough for the three of them to sit on. No faces. No drama. Just that image.

On the opposite page, where Gwen usually wrote her visions, there was only one word:

GO.

Kate reached over and gently closed the cover.

The sisters sat together on the couch, the morning sun warm through the window, the air quiet around them. Everything Gwen had seen. Everything she had left behind.

The journey was only beginning.

Behind them, John sniffled quietly. He had been listening the whole time, eyes glassy, arms folded over his chest.

"She only wrote 'GO'?" Milda said, a little louder than she intended. "That's it? What kind of help is that? Just go? Go where? When?"

Kate and Larissa looked at each other. They knew. Gwen didn't need to say more. The message was clear.

John stood from his desk and stepped into the room, his voice hoarse. "She's telling you to go through the portal. To your mother's world."

No one argued. Not even Milda.

They just sat there, together, letting the weight of it settle around them.

The rest of the day was peaceful, uneventful. Everyone felt like they could use a down day. Milda had taken Gwen's Journal and was rereading for the fourth time at the dining room table. She was scarfing down her third piece of toast and strawberry jam. John was in the kitchen making her a fourth. Kate was in the Kitchen as well stirring dinner since John was busy catering to Milda. Larissa sat next to Milda at the table working on a puzzle. Bob was under the table snoring. He had taken to laying on Larissa's feet whenever he got the chance.

Milda was inspecting the sketches and was finding strange figures with blurred faces, shadows outlined in glowing light, captions and notes in the corners bordered on cryptic poetry.

Milda stopped suddenly, her fingers froze mid-turn.

"Wait, guys, look at this page. These two are in the background of like… every sketch."

Larissa leans in, brushing toast crumbs off the page. Kate comes out of the kitchen leaning over the girls for a better look.

On the page was a charcoal sketch. Two figures standing side by side. One tall and lean, the other broader, solid. Their faces weren't detailed, but their stances were unmistakable—alert, prepared, coiled with tension. A scribbled note underneath read:

"They watch from the edges. Loyal for now. But the wind will change."

Milda flips to another page. Larissa, a puzzle piece in hand, points at the figures on the current page, "They're always watching. Never doing anything, just… there."

The drawing shows a market scene, kids playing, but in the background, two shadowy figures stand near an alley. They appear again in a forest sketch, then in a school hallway.

Turning the page Milda grabs the piece of toast John has just put in front of her. "They look like spies. Or maybe vampires."

Kate, half-laughing, "Pretty sure vampires don't wear Converse."

Milda flips ahead. Another drawing: the same two figures, a bit more detailed now. One taller with short-cropped hair, the other broader, hair pulled back. Still no names. Just shadows with faces.

Larissa, stopped Milda from turning the page, frowning, "Wait a second... They look like the two that were arguing with Dillan, do you remember Milda?"

"Where did you see Dillan arguing with people?" Kate had stood up, straightening her back after leaning over the girls too long starring at the Journal.

Milda leaned into the Journal a bit, "Yeah, they look like that guy and girl Dillan was fighting with, remember they were pointing at us?"

"Where was I when this was happening? Kate had moved around the table facing the girls.

"Oh and there is that creepy cat next to them in this picture" Larissa started flipping to other pages looking for the cat.
Kate put her hands on their shoulders to make sure they heard her, "Exactly when did you see Dillan arguing with people?"

"You were in getting sandwiches, at the Deli" Milda added.

"How come I didn't see him?"

"He was on the side street; he was probably on his break. Is he the reason we have had sandwich from that deli almost every day?" Milda shoved the last piece of toast in her mouth and closed the book with a snap.

"What? No! I love that deli; I eat there all the time." Kate was a bit embarrassed and had no real reason other than wanting to run into Dillan.

Larissa chuckled, "Well I don't know about you Milda, but I am all Ham and Provolone sandwiched out, so Kate either needs to make it official, or Dillan needs a job at a Mexican restaurant for a while."

Milda, jumped up on her chair and spun towards the kitchen, "Chips and

Salsa! John! Do we have any chips and salsa?"

Kate sat down at the table, contemplating why Dillan would be arguing with two figures that were in Gwen's visions. And not in one but seven separate visions. But they didn't seem to belong in any of them. She absently started flipping through the journal.

"And Dillan was arguing with them?"

Larissa had gone back to her puzzle. "We didn't hear the whole thing, but when they walked past the car one of them said something like… 'It's time to take her down.'"

Kate's expression darkened. "And you didn't tell me?"

Milda put her toast back on her plate, whipping her hands on her shirt, crumbs flying,

"You like Dillan. And it sounded like spy stuff. We didn't want to ruin sandwich day."

Kate sighed, rubbing a hand across her forehead, and flipping through the journal with the other. "But they're in here. Gwen knew about them. Said they're loyal 'for now'… That means they were with Eleanor."

Milda, pointing a jam covered finger at the caption "it says 'for now', so maybe not forever?"

Kate was quiet for a long moment, her eyes on the shadowy sketch.

"Maybe not. But if they were planted like Carol was…"

She trailed off. Nobody needed to finish the sentence.

Kate flipped another page, more cautiously this time, as though the journal might snap shut like a trap.

"Wait, look here" Kate motioned for Milda to take a look at the page. "Isn't that the same bird?"

Milda leaned in for a closer look. "Yeah, that is the same type of bird that squawked at me in front of the orphanage.

Kate leaned her head back a bit. "I think it is THE same bird. It is also the same bird that flew around in the courtyard at work, and I have never seen that kind of bird any where".

Larissa chimed in, "black bird with red feathers, has a purple ring around its neck?"

Kate turned towards Larissa, "Yeah, that's it."

Larissa popped another piece of the puzzle in place, "Yeah, I have seen it a couple times too."

Kate continued to flip through the pages, and found two more pictures with the bird in the background. She continued through the book several more times, finding nothing more that would shed any light, she closed the book.

The rest of the night was like the afternoon, calm and uneventful. Kate could not shake the feeling that Dillan may not be the good guy. Bob jumped up on the couch where Kate was sitting and put his head on Kate's lap. It wasn't long before Bob was snoring. Kate laid her head back and closed her eyes. She had had enough thinking for the day.

Thirty-One

More Company

The path curved gently along the ridge, dappled in afternoon light that filtered through the thick canopy above. Jack adjusted the strap of his pack across his chest and glanced behind them.

It was still there.

The creature had been following them for the better part of an hour—silent, cautious, never closer than a dozen yards. Its long limbs moved with eerie grace, blending into the underbrush like a shadow pretending to be flesh.

Kris followed Jack's gaze and whispered, "It's not leaving."

Jack gave a small shake of his head. "Nope. And I think it has company."

Kris turned just in time to see a second figure rise from a slope to their left, just beyond the edge of the trail. This one was slightly smaller, moving with a strange hunch, as if crawling upright. It didn't make a sound as it crept forward to join the first.

Zara, the sleek gray cat riding in the open flap of Kris's coat, let out a lazy yawn and licked one paw. She didn't even glance at the creatures.

"How is she not freaking out?" Kris murmured.

"She's either brave or very dumb," Jack said, forcing a dry chuckle. "I'm hoping for brave."

Kris reached out and grabbed his arm. "Jack."

He followed her gaze.

Ahead, just off the path where the trees thinned into open scrub, a third creature stood waiting. Its posture was different—upright, alert, and still. It didn't approach, didn't move at all, just watched.

The three creatures now formed a triangle—one behind, one to the side, and one ahead.

Kris gripped the strap of her satchel tightly. "Too many, Jack."

Jack nodded grimly. "Yeah. If they wanted to attack, they would've by now. But this feels like something else."

Kris's brow furrowed. "Like what?"

"I don't know," he admitted. "A test? A warning? An escort?"

Zara purred softly.

The forest had gone completely quiet.

Jack and Kris slowed their steps as they neared the third creature.

It stood like a statue, just off the edge of the path—its elongated body barely moving, skin like bark stretched over wiry muscle. The head was tilted slightly, as if listening to something only it could hear. Its eyes, dark and reflective, tracked their approach but made no move to stop them.

Kris's heart pounded in her ears. She could feel the sweat on her palms, but she kept walking.

So did Jack.

They passed within arm's reach.

The creature didn't flinch. It merely turned its head, slowly, following their movement with deliberate curiosity. Zara finally looked up from her perch, blinked once at the creature, and then curled back into Kris's coat.

When they were several steps past, Jack dared to glance over his shoulder.

The creature had stepped onto the path.

It fell in line behind the other two without a sound—three pale shapes drifting silently through the forest at a careful distance.

"They're not hunting us," Jack said under his breath. "They're… following us."

Kris shook her head. "Why? Why now?"

"I don't know. But I think they want to see where we're going."

"Or they already know."

The forest opened ahead, the trees thinning around a bend. The air felt different—brighter, cleaner, like a breeze sweeping out of nowhere. Jack tightened his grip on the strap across his chest.

"We're close to the portal," he said quietly.

Zara raised her head again, eyes narrowing into slits.

The third creature let out a soft, resonant hum—almost like a sigh.

They all kept walking.

Thirty-Two

Doctors orders

D illan waited in the car outside Kate's apartment, the engine idling softly. His fingers tapped the steering wheel as he watched the front door. It had been a long night, and an even longer morning.

Kate stepped out, pulling the door shut behind her. She looked tired but composed. Her hair was damp, she wore a sweatshirt clearly for comfort.

As she approached the car, Milda's voice rang out from the door behind her. "Wait! Kate! Take me with you!"

Kate turned, shaking her head. "Not this time."

"But I can be quiet! I swear—like a shadow. You won't even know I'm there."

Kate gave her a soft smile, her tone final. "I need a break from the commentary. Just this once."

Milda pouted dramatically. "Fine. But if Carol turns out to be an alien shapeshifter or something, I want to know immediately!"

Kate gave a short laugh and waved, then climbed into the passenger seat.

As they pulled away from the curb, Dillan glanced at her. "You sure she's not hiding in the trunk?"

"Checked it twice."

They rode in silence for a minute, the city passing by outside the windows.

Then Dillan asked, "Have you given any more thought to leaving tomorrow?"

Kate nodded. "We're going."

He arched a brow, surprised by the certainty in her voice.

She continued, "The last page of Gwen's journal. There was a drawing. Of the meadow. The stump. And only one word: 'GO.' We're going to follow the journey laid out for us."

Dillan was quiet for a long time. "She saw that far ahead?"

"She saw us reading it. Exactly as we were. It was very creepy seeing her drawing of the exact moment we were in." Kate's voice was quiet but calm. "She knew we'd make this choice."

Dillan gave a slow nod. "Then it is settled."

Kate turned toward him, her face shadowed by the questions she'd been holding in. "What's the other world like? Where we're going. What does it feel like, to go through the portal?"

He smiled faintly. "Like stepping through warm water and landing in a dream you forgot you were having. It pulls at you. Tugs you out of your body for a breath and then gives it back—only changed."

Kate stared out the window for a moment. "What's the other world like?"

Dillan smiled faintly. "It's breathtaking. Ancient forests and floating islands. Cities built into trees and mountains. Magic woven into the very air. It's more alive than anything here. But… it's also more dangerous. Rules are different. Alliances shift. You'll see beauty and turmoil in equal measure."

Kate leaned back, processing that. "And… the punishment for my mother and father. You said it was death. Are they going to try to kill me? And Larissa?"

Dillan's hands tightened slightly on the steering wheel. "No one knows who you are. Not unless you start lighting things on fire or floating over town square." He gave her a sidelong glance. "Don't do that."

"I'll try."

"But yes," he continued, "it's risky. The world we're returning to has changed since your parents left. The council may be fractured. Alliances have shifted. The only thing I can promise is that I will do everything in my power to keep you safe."

Kate stared out the window, watching as the hospital came into view. "That's not enough to make it safe."

"No," Dillan agreed. "But it's enough to make it worth the risk."

They parked, and Kate exhaled deeply before opening her door. Dillan met her as she was getting out, closed the car door, and took her hand.

Together, hand in hand they walked into the hospital. The elevator ride to the third floor was filled with lingering looks and sideways glances as the newness of their relationship was overpowering the severity of their other world situation. The elevator doors opened, reality flowed back between them, they let go of each other's hand.

The hallway was quiet except for the occasional beep and hum of distant monitors. Kate and Dillan stepped into Carol's hospital room.

Carol was dressed and packed, her duffel bag slung over one shoulder. She looked up from tying her shoes and grinned.

"Finally! You're here."

Kate blinked. "Wait—are you… leaving? Are you okay to leave?"

Carol gave a dramatic shrug. "Doctor said I was healing nicely. That's close enough to 'you're good to go' in my book."

Dillan raised an eyebrow. "Did he actually say you could leave?"

Carol shrugged, "Ah. Life is about interpretation."

Carol headed out the hospital room and briskly down the hallway towards the elevator. Kate and Dillan in tow.

Reaching the elevator and waiting for the door to open, a nurse called from behind the desk at the end of the hall.

"Ma'am! You haven't been discharged yet! You need to fill out your paperwork—and the doctor hasn't cleared you" The door opened Carol walked in turning to make a floor selection from the panel as Dillan and Kate found their spot in the elevator.

Carol didn't look up from selecting the button. "He said I was healing nicely! That's practically a marching order."

Dillan shook his head with a slight smirk as the elevator door closed. Kate couldn't help but smile too, the nurse's protests fading as the elevator headed down.

They proceeded out the hospital exit, headed towards the car, the tension of the coming journey beginning to settle on all of them.

Carol sat in the back seat, her hospital bag at her feet, eyes scanning the world outside the window like she hadn't seen it in years. Kate watched her through the rear view mirror, still trying to reconcile the Carol she knew with the woman now pulled into their tangled family mystery. Dillan kept his gaze on the road, a calm anchor in a storm of unknowns.

"So," Carol finally said, breaking the silence. "We're really doing this."

"We are," Kate replied.

"How long do we have?"

Dillan glanced at the clock on the dashboard. "Tomorrow morning. First light, we leave."

Carol gave a low whistle. "Then I hope you all like coffee. There won't be any sleeping tonight."

"Good thing we've had plenty of practice with that lately," Kate said with a dry smile.

Dillan chuckled softly, his fingers tapping the steering wheel. "I'll make a fresh pot when we get back."

"Look at you two," Carol said, leaning forward between the front seats with a mischievous grin. "Finishing each other's thoughts already."

Kate glanced sideways at Dillan, who met her gaze with a soft, knowing smile. There was something unspoken in the look—an acknowledgment of everything they'd been through, and everything they were still figuring out. The corners of Kate's lips tugged upward despite herself.

"Oh my God," Carol laughed, pointing a finger at them. "Was that a look? That was totally a look. You two are *so* obvious."

Kate rolled her eyes, but her cheeks were pink. "Carol, you've been out of the hospital for ten minutes."

"And already doing God's work," Carol said, sitting back smugly. "Just trying to keep things lively."

Dillan didn't say anything, but the amused twitch of his mouth gave him away.

The car slowed as they turned onto a quiet street. Kate's apartment complex came into view, lights in the windows glowing soft and golden.

"Well," Dillan said, pulling up to the curb, "this is us."

Carol stretched and reached for her bag. "Okay, lovers, try not to make too much eye contact on the way to the door. Someone might faint from the tension."

Kate shot her a playful glare as she opened her door. Dillan chuckled and shook his head, then slipped out, grabbing the bag from Carol as she shot him a grin and punched him in the arm.

The smell of leftover pizza from last nights dinner hung in the air . The apartment was warmer than Carol expected. It was filled with the kind of quiet that followed long, hard truths.

Milda was sprawled on the floor with a notebook, doodling lightning bolts and flowers in alternating patterns. She looked up and gasped when she saw Carol.

"You escaped!" she grinned, launching to her feet. "I was betting you'd sneak out in a laundry cart."

"Not far off," Carol said. "But I walked. Like a rebel."

John appeared from the hallway, raising an eyebrow at the sight of Carol's bag.

"She's staying," Kate said simply.

John nodded once. "Then we better make dinner. We've got a long night ahead."

The girls exchanged glances.

John was in the kitchen, chopping vegetables with mechanical precision. He had the air of someone who needed something to do with his hands, and feeding a group about to throw themselves into danger seemed like the right outlet.

"Stir-fry okay? Lots of fresh vegetables," he asked without looking up.

"Perfect," Kate said. She looked over at Carol, who had already settled on a stool at the kitchen island. "You okay?"

Carol shrugged. "Doctor said I was healing nicely."

"That's not the same as 'cleared to leave,'" Dillan said dryly.

Carol smirked. "Close enough."

Milda popped up beside the fridge. "Wait, did you even sign discharge papers?"

From down the hall, they could still hear a nurse's distant voice yelling about incomplete forms and needing the doctor's final sign-off.

Dillan laughed under his breath. "Well, she's gone now. Too late."

As the aroma of garlic and simmering sauce filled the kitchen, John wiped his hands on a kitchen towel and turned to face them all. "I'm coming with you."

The words hung in the air.

No one argued. Kate smiled.

"Good," she said. "We need you."

Dillan glanced at the clock. "I need to go pack. I'll be back in the morning, no later than 8. Be ready. It is a half a day car ride and another couple hours walk to the portal site."

Carol nodded. "I'll be ready too. Just need to swing by the warehouse after dinner. I've got some gear stashed there."

Kate looked up. "I'll go with you."

"Hey! What about us?" Milda asked. "Larissa and I aren't just going to sit here while you go off adventuring."

"You need rest," Kate started, but Larissa was already shaking her head.

"I've seen it," she said firmly. "We all need to go."

Kate squinted at her. "You know, if you were just making this stuff up, none of us would ever know."

Larissa smiled slightly. "That's the fun part."

After dinner, they would head to the warehouse. Then… they'd be ready.

Thirty-Three

Here we go again

The warehouse looked like a battlefield, forgotten and frozen in time. Debris still littered the floor from their last confrontation. A fight that had seemed like a lifetime ago, though only days had passed. The air was thick with dust and memory.

Carol led the way, her boots crunching over broken glass as she navigated toward a collapsed shelving unit in the corner. She crouched and began rummaging through the wreckage, pulling out tools, a coil of wire, and a small, dented metal box, all of which she began to tuck into her backpack.

"I'm really surprised my mother hasn't shown up," she said, her voice low but heavy with concern. "Do you think she's given up?"

Milda, standing near a toppled cabinet, puffed her chest and declared, "Maybe she's still nursing her wounds from the epic butt-kicking I gave her."

Kate laughed, and even Carol cracked a smile. But Larissa only gave a faint, distant smile, her eyes drifting across the dim space.

A ripple of cold moved through the air.

From behind them, a voice sliced through the warehouse like a dagger. "I didn't think you'd be stupid enough to come back here."

They turned as one. Eleanor stood near the entrance, her presence commanding and venomous as ever. Her dark coat trailed behind her like a shadow come to life.

"But what a stroke of luck," she continued, her voice thick with malice. "Now I can kill all of you and still make it to the portal in time."

Carol rose slowly, fists clenched. Kate stepped in front of Milda and Larissa, her breath catching in her chest.

This time, they were ready.

Eleanor's eyes brightened with a devious idea. She looked above them, and a smile crossed her face. She pointed her hands toward a giant light fixture overhead, snapping the bracing. The light swung down behind them, and Eleanor focused on the floor again, trying to keep the girls off-balance.

Larissa knew the danger was coming and shouted, "Duck!"

The girls dropped instinctively, but as they got up, the light swung back toward them. Milda was in the path, and neither Kate nor Milda had noticed. Larissa, however, pushed Milda out of the way, taking the full force of the light across her chest. She flew through the air and crashed into some crates twenty feet away.

Carol sprang into action, moving between Eleanor and the others, started fending off crates and debris and sending them back in her mothers direction. Eleanor deflected them with a swipe of her hand, her attention momentarily split.

Milda, became infuriated seeing her sister on the ground. "No more!" Milda motioned, summoning an air conditioning unit that came unbolted from the floor and flew toward Eleanor. Eleanor stopped it mid-air, her focus solely on stopping Milda's attack. Everything else dropped to the ground.

"You won't be able to stop me!" Eleanor screamed. "You're no match for me. I can already feel your power faltering, though I must admit, for six, you have quite the gift."

"I'm seven, you sack of cow poop!" Milda's fists clenched tighter, her hair floating wildly.

Kate moved to Larissa's side, her hands on her. Larissa was alive but barely responsive. "I'm fine, help Milda!" Larissa's voice wavered.

"You're not fine!" Kate's panic was clear as she assessed Larissa's condition.

She could feel the broken bones, the bruising, and the internal injuries but couldn't quite tell what else was wrong. That terrified her more than anything.

"If you don't help Milda, we're all going to die." Kate couldn't pull away from Larissa. The words were choked with emotion.

Carol glanced back at them and then lunged forward again, summoning a length of pipe from the debris and whipping it toward Eleanor. The pipe missed as Eleanor swerved, but it gave Milda just enough time to redirect her energy and send Eleanor skidding backward across the floor.

"I'm not letting you hurt them again!" Carol yelled, voice trembling with fury.

Eleanor rose slowly, brushing dust from her coat, eyes narrowing as she took in all three girls and Carol standing, bloodied but unyielding.

As Eleanor raised her hands above her head a black bird swooped down and clawed at her right hand. Eleanor pulled her hand to her chest and scanned the room frantically looking for something or someone. She stopped and starred directly at the girls.

Eleanor's face had gone white, "NO!" she screamed.

The girls had not seen a cloaked figure walking up behind them until she stepped up and between them.

The figure pulled back her hood, revealing the woman from the photo. Her face was worn but determined. She gave Kate a brief nod.

"Kate, don't leave her side. I'll help Milda and Carol."

Without hesitation, Kate turned back to Larissa, her eyes flicking from her sister to Carol, then to the stranger.

"Eleanor!" the woman shouted, her voice echoing through the warehouse like thunder. "This has gone far enough!"

Eleanor stumbled, stunned. "Genevieve? You're dead! How many times do I have to kill you?"

"Apparently more than three," Genevieve said coolly. "Since the explosion last month didn't do the trick. And yet, here you are, still trying to kill my children."

The black bird swooped through the air again, diving at Eleanor's head.

Genevieve repositioned herself in between Milda and Carol. Milda, still bracing herself against Eleanor's power, looked over and grinned.

"You're doing great," Genevieve whispered to her. "Just a few more minutes. Think you can hang on?"

"I got this!" Milda replied, her voice full of grit.

Genevieve turned back to Eleanor. "It ends now. Walk away."

"This ends when you and your offspring are dead!" Eleanor roared. "You killed my brother. You broke the law. You took my love from me. And you turned my daughter."

"Eleanor, we've all made mistakes. We've all moved on. You need to let it go."

Genevieve let her coat fall from her shoulders to the floor.

"Never!" Eleanor screamed, hurling the a/c unit toward her.

Genevieve raised her hand and caught Milda's shoulder, transferring her strength. "Now, Milda! Let her have it!"

Milda felt a surge of energy run through her and she launched the unit back toward Eleanor. Eleanor successfully ducked but crates were already flying towards her. Milda's power pulsed through the air. SYeah he was throwing debris in every direction. Eleanor staggered, shielding herself but taking several hits.

"Carol, come here!" Genevieve called.

Carol scrambled over. Genevieve placed a hand on her shoulder, and Carol's eyes lit with sudden strength. Her whole body tensed with renewed purpose.

"I'll never stop!" Eleanor screamed. "I'll find you and your children wherever you go!"

She sent another massive crate hurling toward the group.

Carol dropped her arms to her sides and pressed her palms toward the floor, concentrating. The ground beneath Eleanor cracked and trembled. A fissure split open under her feet.

"Milda, look up," Genevieve said, barely above a whisper.

Milda followed her mother's gaze. Above Eleanor hung a massive steel beam.

Milda grinned. She focused.

For a moment, nothing happened. Then the beam groaned—and the entire roof section above it collapsed.

The steel crashed down with a deafening roar, burying Eleanor beneath rubble and dust.

"Whoa," Milda said, breathless. "I was only aiming for the beam…"

Dust filled the air. The girls coughed, trying to find one another. Milda was already crawling toward Larissa.

"Larissa!" Milda reached her sister and shook her, panic rising. Larissa didn't respond.

"Help her, Kate! Fix her!" Milda sobbed, clutching Kate's hands and pressing them to Larissa's chest.

"I can't…" Kate whispered. "I've already tried. I can't."

She tried to pull away, but Milda held her hands in place.

Genevieve stepped in, placing a hand on Kate's shoulder. "You can do this, Kate. We're here with you." The black bird fluttered down and landed on Genevieve's shoulder.

Carol appeared at Kate's other side, adding her own hand to Kate's shoulder.

Tears streamed down Kate's face. "I tried. I really tried…"

Genevieve leaned closer. "Try again. Milda—help her."

Milda's hair began to float around her head, charged with power. She reached out, gently guiding Kate's hands back onto Larissa's chest. Her eyes closed in concentration. A low hum filled the air.

Heat radiated from Milda's hands into Larissa's body. Kate felt it too—and she focused. She visualized Larissa healing, bones knitting, bruises fading.

The air thickened. The warehouse pulsed with energy.

Finally, the injuries inside Larissa's body began to heal. Kate could sense it. She held for a few moments longer, until she could feel Larissa's body was whole again. She stopped channeling. Milda dropped her hands and began brushing dust from Larissa's face.

They waited in silence.

"Were we too late?" Kate's voice trembled.

"No," Milda said softly. "Her injuries healed—you saw it."

"But maybe it wasn't enough…"

Genevieve gave her a gentle squeeze. "Give her time. A lot of healing happened. She just needs to catch up."

They sat in stillness. Milda reached out and turned Larissa's face toward her.

"You can't die," she whispered. "You have to wake up. We didn't finish our tea party."

Kate let out a sob, pressing her hand to Milda's back. "I'm sorry…"

Then—Larissa's eyelid twitched. The bird squawked.

"Milda, wait," Kate said, holding her breath.

Milda froze.

Larissa groaned, her head tilting toward them. Her voice rasped, faint but unmistakably hers.

"Well… I can't go before we finish the tea party."

Milda burst into laughter; her face still wet with tears. Kate covered her mouth with her hand, crying and laughing all at once.

Larissa looked around at them all, dazed but aware.

"I thought we lost you," Kate whispered, wiping her eyes.

Larissa gave a fragile smile. "Not yet. Don't worry. There's still more to finish."

Larissa sat up slowly with help from Milda and Kate, still weak but smiling, her body trembling with effort.

Genevieve knelt beside her daughters, her expression softening as she gently brushed a lock of hair from Larissa's forehead. "You were incredible. All of you."

Larissa looked up at the woman they had seen only in photos. Her mind struggled to reconcile the face of her dreams with the very real, very present person in front of her.

"You're our mother," Kate said softly.

Genevieve nodded, emotion thick in her throat. "I am. And I've been waiting so long to meet you." The black bird flew off Genevieve's shoulder and landed on the other side of Larissa walking back and forth as if inspecting something.

Larissa put her hand out to him, "does he have a name?"

"Piper" Genevieve said. The black bird jumped into Larissa's hand for a moment and then flew off.

Milda watched the bird fly away and then looked back at Genevieve. "Why now?"

"Because now… you were strong enough. And I couldn't stay hidden any longer. I'm so proud of you." Her voice broke slightly as she gathered them all into a hug, cradling them close like it was the only thing keeping her together.

Carol stood back, watching with wide eyes. Her gaze drifted toward the massive pile of twisted steel and debris that had once been part of the roof— and where her mother had stood just moments before.

"She's gone," Carol said quietly.

They followed her eyes to the wreckage. No sign of Eleanor. Just dust, collapsed beams, and the faint crackle of settling rubble. The entire ceiling had caved in, burying whatever had been in its path.

"No one could survive that," Carol whispered. "Not even her."

"She's gone," Genevieve said gently. "But the cost of her hate lives on in all of us. I'm so sorry, Carol."

Carol nodded slowly. Her mother had tried to kill them all—again—and yet, a part of her still wanted to believe something else had been possible. But not anymore. The silence after the storm was proof enough.

The weight of grief and reunion lingered in the air. It was impossible to tell which feeling was heavier meeting their mother, or losing Carol's.

Genevieve stood, brushing off the dust from her hands. "We don't have long," she said, glancing toward the warehouse's broken windows where the moon was moving across the sky. "Are you ready?"

"We need to get back," Kate said. "Clean up, regroup, get what we need."

"I'll meet you at the portal sight," Genevieve said. "There are still a few things I need to do."

Kate looked concerned. "Will you be safe?"

Genevieve smiled a deep smile. "Yes."

Milda stood up and hugged her mother's legs, still catching her breath. "Don't be late. We've got a new world to get too." Genevieve brushed her hands through Milda's hair.

Carol slung her backpack over her shoulder, her face solemn but steady. "Let's go."

Together, the five of them turned and walked out of the wrecked warehouse. The battle was over. The real journey was about to begin.

Thirty-Four

Calm before the portal

The apartment was quiet, the kind of heavy silence that only follows chaos. Faint streaks of streetlamp light filtered through the living room curtains, casting long shadows across the floor. Dust-streaked, blood-smudged, and exhausted, they barely said a word as they each cleaned up, changed into something comfortable, and collapsed into the nearest available spot.

Carol sat on the couch, her back straight but her body visibly tired. Larissa had curled up beside her, head in Carol's lap, already deep asleep. Her breathing was slow and steady, a small patch of dried blood still matted in her hair, Larissa still too week to properly wash up.

Milda was leaning against Kate on the other end of the couch, her head resting on her sister's shoulder. She was asleep too, though every now and then her face would twitch, as if still fighting something in her dreams.

Kate wasn't asleep. Neither was Carol.

They sat in silence for a long time, the hush wrapping around them like a blanket. The air smelled faintly of soap, dried sweat, and the lingering scent of something burning—maybe it was just a memory.

Carol glanced down at Larissa, brushing a piece of hair from her face. "She's okay?"

Kate nodded, her voice soft. "Yeah, just sleeping."

There was a pause before Kate looked over. "And you? Are *you* okay?"

Carol didn't answer right away. Her eyes drifted to the dark window beyond the curtains. "I don't know, I thought I'd feel something more. Angry or sad maybe relieved.?But I just feel empty."

"She was your mom."

"Yeah. She was." Carol's voice cracked slightly, and she swallowed hard. "She tried to kill me. She tried to kill *you*. Again. And I still want to cry."

"You can," Kate said gently.

Carol blinked a few times. "She loved me, in her own way. I just wish things had been different. I wish she could've let go. Of all of it."

Kate nodded. "We all do."

They sat quietly again. Outside, the city was just beginning to stir, the distant sound of a trash truck groaning its way down the street blending with the occasional bark of a dog or early riser walking past.

"I wonder what the other world will be like?" Kate pondered quietly.

Carol shook her head. "Mom use to tell me about it. She said the sky changed colors, that is was much more vibrant than here. She said there was fire coming out of the ground, rivers of fire."

Kate's eyes lowered. "Do you think it's still like that?"

"I don't know," Carol whispered. "But I don't think we're going back to the same world they left. I worry that we are heading back into a very dangerous situation."

Kate fingers traced small patterns on Milda's arm, comforting herself as much as her sister. "What if we don't belong there?"

Carol let out a soft laugh, bitter but not cold. "Do we belong here?"

Kate met her eyes, and they both nodded slowly. That much, at least, made sense.

The sound of a door creaking open made them both glance toward the hallway.

John emerged, rubbing his eyes beneath his glasses, his flannel shirt wrinkled. He froze when he saw the four of them on the couch, the aftermath of battle written all over their faces.

"Did you sleep at all?" he voice hoarse from a rough nights sleep.

Kate shook her head. "I tried."

He glanced at Carol. She offered a small smile but didn't say anything.

He stood still for a beat longer, wanting to say more, but then nodded slowly.

Without another word, he headed into the kitchen, rolling up his sleeves and flipping on the light. A moment later, the comforting sounds of a coffee grinder buzzed through the silence, followed by the hiss of the stove. Bacon hit the pan with a crackle, and the rich, grounding aroma of breakfast started to fill the room.

"That man is a saint," Carol whispered, her voice barely audible.

Kate smiled. "He really is."

Carol looked down at Milda, then over at Larissa, still peacefully asleep. "Do you think we're going to be okay?"

Kate didn't answer right away. She leaned her head back against the couch, her voice soft but certain.

"I think we're going to try."

Thirty-Five

Road to nowhere

Dillan arrived just before 8 a.m., right on time. The knock at the door was gentle, almost apologetic. When John opened it, Bob bounded inside first, tail wagging, nails scrabbling on the wood floors as he made a beeline for the couch.

"Bob!" Milda squealed as Bob nearly knocked her over in his enthusiasm. He barked joyfully and danced around the girls.

"You missed us, huh?" Larissa grinned, rubbing behind his ears.

"I made breakfast if you are hungry" John said quietly to Dillan as he stepped inside.

"Thanks," Dillan replied. He glanced at the girls. "You all ready?"

"Define *ready*," Carol muttered, pulling on her boots.

Milda stood in the middle of the living room surrounded by no fewer than four bags. Bob bouncing between each of them sniffing the contents. "Okay. I'm bringing these three… and maybe this one."

Kate arched a brow. "That's not happening."

"But what if I need my art stuff? Or snacks? Or backup snacks? What if they don't have *blankets* in the new world?"

"You get *one* bag, Milda," Kate said, not unkindly. "and you are carrying it."

Milda groaned but started repacking with theatrical despair. "You people have no vision."

Loading the car took longer than expected thanks to Milda's last-minute wardrobe crisis and Bob's tendency to jump into the front seat. But eventually, everything was crammed in, and they were all on their way.

The ride started quiet. No one mentioned the portal. No one brought up Eleanor. Carol sat by the window, her head leaning against the glass, watching the city fade behind them. Kate was on the other window in the back, with Larissa and Milda squeezed in the middle. Bob laid happily over their laps, his tongue lolling out the side of his mouth. John was shotgun, leaving Dillan to driving since he was the only one who knew where they were going.

"I spy with my little eye…" Milda began about twenty minutes in, and the game was on.

Larissa won. Every time.

"That's not fair," Carol protested with a smirk. "You're literally *seeing things before they happen.*"

"I *only* use my powers for evil," Larissa said dramatically, hand over her heart.

"Let's do another round," Milda said, trying to distract from the quiet that always threatened to slip back in. "But this time, Bob gets to guess."

Bob barked. No one was entirely sure whether it was a yes or a protest.

After the laughter faded again, Milda rested her chin on the back of Dillan's seat and asked the question that had been building behind her teeth for hours. "What is my mom like?"

Dillan didn't answer right away. The road hummed beneath the tires as they turned onto a smaller, more secluded road.

"She is kind," he said eventually. "And fierce. And smart. The kind of smart that makes you nervous. And she loved you all fiercely. She will do anything to protect you girls."

"Why didn't she come back for us sooner?"

"She tried," Dillan said softly. "But staying together was too dangerous. Eleanor was watching. If Genevieve had stayed near you, it would have been like lighting a beacon."

Milda was quiet for a moment. "So she had to let us go… to keep us safe?"
Dillan nodded once.

"I think I get it," Milda said. "I don't like it. But I get it."

The silence that followed wasn't heavy. It was thoughtful. Larissa leaned her head against Kate and closed her eyes.

Kate, watching Dillan in the rear view mirror, decided it was her turn for twenty questions. "So… how old *are* you, anyway?" starting with one that Dillan had been dodging.

Dillan didn't blink. He kept his eyes on the road.

"I mean, you act like you've been around forever." Kate turned toward Carol. "Do you know how old he is?"

"Well, he came through the portal eighty years ago" Carol said calmly.

Milda sat up straighter and spun to face Carol. "Wait—what?"

Carol moved the hair out of Milda's face, "We age very slowly after puberty, so we look a lot younger than humans our age"

Kate raised an eyebrow, trying to put the puzzle together. "In the picture we saw at the warehouse, he looked the same as he does now and that would have had to be on the other planet?"

"Yep" Carol confirmed.

"*What?*" Milda shrieked. "He's, like, a hundred? That's… ew! That's old!"

Dillan cracked a grin but still didn't answer. Bob barked once, as if laughing with them.

Eventually, the car turned down a dirt road so narrow that branches scratched softly against the windows. After several more minutes, the vehicle rolled to a slow stop.

There were no buildings. No signs. No path.

"Uh… are we lost?" Milda asked, peering out the window.

"Nope," Dillan said. "We're here."

Kate opened her door and stepped out, the earth beneath her boots damp with morning dew. A thick forest stretched before them—dense, overgrown, and untouched.

Carol stared. "There's no trail."

"We don't need one," Dillan said. "We walk straight through. No stops. No shortcuts. Middle of nowhere. That's where the portal is."

Larissa climbed out and slung her bag over her shoulder. "Well, that sounds ominous."

Milda wrinkled her nose. "You sure you don't want to *pave* the way or something first?"

Dillan started unpacking the trunk, "Not how this works."

They all began shouldering their bags in silence, the soft rustle of leaves and the distant call of birds, the only sounds around them. Bob bounded ahead, tail wagging, already thrilled by the adventure.

One by one, they stepped into the woods.

There was no turning back now.

Thirty-Six

Thru the trees

The forest swallowed them whole within minutes. Sunlight filtered through the canopy in dappled gold, casting long shadows across mossy roots and tangled underbrush. Birds chattered above, and the soft squelch of boots on damp earth became the rhythm of their journey.

Bob trotted ahead, nose to the ground, occasionally darting off after a smell before circling back like a shaggy scout. Dillan led with confident steps, navigating the wild terrain as if he'd walked this path a thousand times. John brought up the rear, his backpack strapped tight, quietly watching everyone's backs.

Milda, predictably, was the first to break the peace.

"Oh! Look at these!" she gasped, darting off to the side and plucking a handful of purple flowers. "Larissa, do you think these are poisonous?"

"Only one way to find out," Larissa said dryly, stepping over a root.

Milda sniffed them suspiciously. "They smell like bubblegum and doom. I'll call them *Doomblooms.*"

"Please don't put those in your mouth," Kate muttered.

They walked for another ten minutes in near silence before Milda piped up again.

"Okay, new topic: Dillan's age. I think he's, like… 97."

"Nope," Dillan said without looking back.

"Okay. 121?"

"Wrong again."

"150?"

"Still not it."

"Come on, give me a hint!"

Larissa, without breaking stride, said, "You're not even close."

Kate stopped in her tracks. "Wait. *Older?* You knew that?"

Larissa shrugged. "I just saw it. Like… a number, kind of floating over his head. Weird. It's a lot."

Dillan glanced over his shoulder and raised an eyebrow at her. "You're getting stronger."

Kate frowned. "Okay, hold up. What do you mean 'a lot'? Like, 200?"

Larissa looked at Dillan, then back at Kate. "Try starting with a 3.."

"What?!" Milda nearly tripped on a vine. "He's 300 *years old*?! Dillan! That is… *ancient.* That's *pre-plumbing.* That's like… you're older than some mountains!"

"I still have better knees than John," Dillan said, glancing back with a smirk.

"I *heard* that," John called from behind, though he didn't sound offended.

Kate's face was pale. "Wait, if *he* doesn't age like us… then… does that mean *we* won't?"

Larissa was quiet for a moment. "I don't think we will. At least… not like humans do. We're different."

Carol nodded solemnly. "We were always different. You just didn't know yet."

Larissa looked over her shoulder at John, walking alone at the back of the line. He smiled at her when he noticed her gaze, but her chest tightened all the same.

He wouldn't age like them. He wouldn't go where they were going.

But no one said it out loud.

Bob suddenly stopped and gave a low whine, his ears perked forward.

"What is it, boy?" Milda whispered, crouching beside him.

They followed his gaze through the thick trees.

Up ahead, quite a distance away and mostly obscured by the shifting forest, something moved.

It was tall—*too* tall—and pale, its limbs bending at strange angles as it slipped between the trees. It didn't look toward them. Didn't change direction. Just... moved. As if it were traveling the same way they were.

"What is that?" Carol asked softly.

Kate narrowed her eyes. "It doesn't seem to notice us... but it definitely doesn't look friendly."

"Should we hide?" Milda whispered.

"No," Dillan said, voice steady. "If it wanted to come for us, it already would have. Just keep walking."

They obeyed, but every one of them kept glancing sideways through the trees, watching the pale shape until it disappeared behind the thickets.

Milda finally muttered, "Okay, new plan: when we get to the new world, *no tall creepy forest people.*"

"No promises," Dillan said.

"Seriously?" Milda groaned.

"Can't we just get one *normal* day?" Kate added.

"No," Larissa, Carol, and Dillan all said at once.

Bob barked like he agreed.

They pressed deeper into the woods—toward the unknown, toward the portal, and toward the lives they were only just beginning to live.

Thirty-Seven

The Clearing

The forest began to thin.

Morning light had turned into afternoon and spread wider now, glinting off dew-covered leaves as they approached a break in the trees. But before the group reached the edge, Larissa stopped.

"There," she said, pointing through the trunks.

Two more creatures. Pale, spindly, and unnaturally tall. Their elongated limbs swayed slightly as they walked, not toward the group, but *with* them—keeping pace just far enough away to remain out of reach.

"That's three of them," Kate murmured. "And they're all going the same direction."

"They're following the same pull," John said, adjusting his pack. "Same as us."

Milda stepped closer to Bob, placing a hand on his back. "They give me the creeps… but they don't feel dangerous."

Dillan's face was carved in stone. He didn't say anything. He just kept walking. The trees began to fall around them.

And then, they were out.

The forest opened wide into a vast, sweeping meadow, the golden grass moving like waves in a silent sea. The sky stretched high above them, blue and cloudless, the wind carrying the faint scent of flowers and something older—earthy and strange.

In the distance, across the wide clearing, they saw them.

Figures. Many of them.

Carol squinted. "Those aren't just Kris and Jack."

Dillan stopped dead in his tracks. "No. It should *only* be Kris, Jack, and Genevieve."

Everyone froze.

Far ahead, about a dozen creatures stood scattered through the meadow—some towering like trees, others smaller and hunched. Their pale skin shimmered faintly under the sun. They weren't moving. Just standing. Encircling something at the center of the clearing.

Kris and Jack.

Both were sitting calmly on the large tree stump, like two kids waiting for a bus. Zara was lying down between them without an thought of being surrounded by nightmarish creatures.

"What are they doing?" Kate breathed.

"They don't look scared," Carol said, stepping forward.

Dillan didn't respond. His jaw tightened as he scanned the field. "Something's off."

Bob growled low in his throat, staying close to Milda's leg.

"are we sure that is Kris and Jack?" Milda asked, ever curious.

Carol never taking her eyes off the scene, "we will find out soon enough"

"Wait—look!" Larissa pointed toward the far end of the field. "There's someone coming."

They all looked in the direction Larissa was pointing.

A figure—human, unmistakably—walked slowly toward Kris and Jack from the other side of the clearing. A woman. Her hair caught the wind, long and dark. She walked with purpose. Not afraid. Not hurried.

"Is it...?" Milda's voice caught.

Her hand pressed against her chest. Hope surged behind her eyes.

"Is that my mom?" Milda asked, breath held tight in her chest.

No one answered.

The figure grew closer, her features still obscured by distance.

But then, the creatures began to move.

Slowly at first. Subtle shifts in posture. Turning. Repositioning. Forming a line *between* Kris and Jack and the approaching woman.

The three that had been in step with them started picking up speed, hurrying towards the others.

"But, where is Piper?" Milda squinted to see if maybe the bird was in the air.

A sudden, sharp *crack* echoed through the field as one of the smaller creatures was lifted violently into the air and hurled against one of the towering ones. The impact sounded like bone on stone. Another followed— lifted, thrown, like a rag doll into its kin.

Kris and Jack sprang up from the stump, dropping into defensive stances. Zara raised up her hair standing on end.

"What's happening?" Kate gasped.

Dillan's voice was cold and rough. "That's not Genevieve."

Kate squinted, stepping forward. Her eyes widened. "It's Eleanor. She's *alive.*"

Another creature was picked up and slammed into the ground hard enough to shake the grass for yards.

"She's using them—she's *controlling* them!" Carol shouted.

"No," Dillan corrected grimly. "She's using them as *weapons.*"

The creatures weren't attacking. They were defending—circling Kris and Jack in a protective shield, some stepping in front, others bracing for impact.

"She's trying to break through them" Carol said, panic rising in her voice.

"We have to help them—*now!*" Dillan broke into a run, Carol right behind him.

Kate turned to the others. "Stay close. Protect each other."

"Bob, go!" Milda pointed, and the dog tore after Dillan and Carol, sprinting ahead with surprising speed and a low growl building in his chest.

The girls ran behind them, all of them watching Eleanor as they ran. Elanor raised one hand into the air. Larissa motioned toward Eleanor, "Look, what is she doing?"

And as if in response, the sky began to darken.

Something was coming.

The sky shimmered like the heat coming off a hot metal roof. A low hum vibrated through the meadow, rising higher in pitch, matching the pulse in Kate's ears.

Dillan and Carol were nearly to the edge of the circle of creatures, ducking under flailing limbs as Eleanor hurled smaller beings into the larger ones with telekinetic precision. Her face, was twisted with rage and something worse, desperation.

Kris and Jack stood at the center of the chaos, back-to-back, eyes darting between the moving creatures and the oncoming storm that was Eleanor.

"She's going to tear through them," Dillan muttered as he slid to a stop beside a towering stone beast that had taken a blow to the shoulder.

Carol raised her hands, drawing in the ambient energy around her. The ground beneath them pulsed once, and the air buzzed with static. "Not if we stop her first."

Eleanor saw them, her eyes locked on Carol. "You! You traitor!" she bellowed. "You were supposed to be with me!"

She swept her hand out and a chunk of earth tore up from the meadow, flying at Carol. Dillan shoved Carol aside, the mass slamming into his side with a dull *crack* before he collapsed to one knee.

"DILL!" Carol screamed, skidding to his side.

"I'm fine—go!" he growled. Bob ran to Dillan's side whimpering but keeping guard.

Kate and the girls arrived just as Eleanor raised both arms, lifting multiple creatures into the air at once. The portal site pulsed behind her, still dormant, but its energy was beginning to stir.

"Stop her!" Kris shouted, dodging a crashing creature that slammed to the ground inches from her feet. Zara had just narrowly jumped from her side.

Milda moved without thinking, throwing her hands forward. A gust of pressure shot toward Eleanor, knocking her off balance just long enough for the lifted creatures to fall—harmlessly this time.

Larissa ran to Jack's side. "Are you okay?"

Jack nodded. "She came out of nowhere. We thought she was Genevieve until it was too late. The creatures were just *here*. They started protecting us."

"Why?" Larissa asked.

"I think they're tied to the portal."

Kate turned to Carol. "Can we overpower her? Like before?"

Carol looked uncertain. "She's stronger now. Angrier. But if we're together…"

Eleanor shrieked, voice unnatural. "You *can't* stop me! This is *my* legacy!

A blinding blast of energy burst from her chest—wild, feral. It struck several creatures, sending them sprawling. One flew backward, colliding with the tree line behind them.

Milda gritted her teeth, grounding herself. "We do it like we did with Larissa."

Carol nodded. "Together."

They moved in sync—Kate, Milda, Carol, and Larissa—hands linked, energy pooling between them. The air glowed gold, pulsing with heartbeats, emotion, connection.

Eleanor stepped forward, dragging her feet as if walking through syrup. "You think love will save you?"

"No," Kate said calmly. "But it's going to destroy *you*."

They unleashed it.

The blinding blast of energy struck Eleanor full force—light blooming outward, not just power, but *memory*. Fragments of her past flickered behind her eyes. love, loss, betrayal, the child she'd turned, the brother she'd lost, and her Alexander.

She screamed—not in pain, but in something worse. Recognition. Regret. And then she *fell*.

The wind died. The pressure eased.

Eleanor's body hit the ground with a heavy thud. Dust curled around her motionless form. She lay in a tangle of limbs and black fabric, eyes open but unfocused, chest barely rising.

Not gone.

But down.

A ripple of silence passed through the clearing. The creatures, battered and bruised, slowly relaxed. One let out a low rumble, half-growl, half-sigh, as it backed away from Kris and Jack.

Dillan had managed to get to his feet. Bob would not leave his side.

Then Larissa pointed, breath catching. "There."

Across the far end of the field, a figure approached, with a bird flying overhead.

This time, it was her.

Genevieve.

Walking toward them, cloak catching the wind, her steps sure and calm.

Milda gasped. "Mom?", Milda broke into a run.

"MOM!" she cried, full tilt across the grass, arms out. Piper flew out and around Milda as she ran.

Genevieve barely had time to steady herself before Milda barreled into her, wrapping her in a fierce, tearful hug. The rest of the group followed quickly, slower but no less moved. Kate, Larissa, and Carol joined the embrace one by one, and Genevieve pulled them close, her hands trembling against the backs of their heads.

"I knew you'd make it," she whispered.

They stood like that for a moment, a fragile circle in the open field.

As they turned and began walking back toward the edge of the forest— toward the faint shimmer of the waiting portal—the creatures stirred behind them. A low ripple of movement rolled through their strange ranks. Then Carol froze.

"Wait," she said quietly. "Where is she?"

They all turned.

Eleanor was gone.

The place where she'd fallen was empty. The tall grass there was crushed, blood smeared in dark rust, but her body had vanished.

Kate folded her arms. "Doesn't matter. She's hurt, she's alone, and she's not coming with us. She can't follow us."

Piper flew down and landed on Genevieve's shoulder, head low.

Genevieve had stopped walking. Her face had changed.

"No," she said softly. "I can't go."

"What?" Kate turned. "Why?"

Genevieve looked at her daughters—each one bruised, weary, but alive. Her voice broke as she said, "Because you have a brother."

Everyone stilled.

"A what?" Milda said, brightening with sudden joy. "A baby brother?!"

"He's not even a year old," Genevieve said, her eyes glistening. "His name is Alder."

Larissa blinked. "Why didn't you bring him with you?"

Before Genevieve could answer, Dillan stepped in, still holding his side. "He's too young. The portal takes a toll on the body. He wouldn't survive it."

Genevieve nodded. "And if Eleanor is still alive… I must stay. I must protect him. He's all alone in this world except for me."

"But she doesn't even know about him," Milda said quickly.

Kris spoke up from the edge of the group, her voice grim. "She does. She just doesn't know where he is… or even that he's a boy. But she knows he exists. She's been looking."

A long silence followed.

Kate opened her mouth to argue, but John stepped forward. "I'm staying too."

"What?" Kate gasped.

"I'll slow you down. I'm not like you. I'm older, I won't live as long. But I can help Genevieve. I can help protect Alder."

"But—" Kate's voice cracked. "You're my dad."

John smiled, stepping forward to cup her cheek. "And that's why I'm doing this. For you, for all of you. So that one day, you'll get to meet your brother. So you'll get to know your mother when she joins you later."

Tears welled in Kate's eyes.

"I'll make sure they're safe," John said, his voice steady.

"I'll help too," Carol said suddenly.

Everyone turned to her.

"I was part of what happened," she said quietly. "I was used. I made mistakes. But I want to make this right. And I'll see you again—in twenty years or so, when the portal opens again. When Alder is strong enough."

Genevieve touched her arm, grateful and surprised. Piper jumped over and landed on carol's shoulder, with a soft twitter.

The goodbyes were quiet, choked with emotion. Long hugs, whispered promises, hands squeezed like lifelines. Kate wept openly but smiled through her tears. Larissa hugged Carol last, their eyes locked with unspoken understanding.

"I'll see you again," Carol said.

"I know." Larissa said with confidence and Carol understood and smiled wide.

And then, Dillan gave the signal.

Kris and Jack moved ahead, Zara marching between them. The portal shimmered just beyond the tree line like a ripple in air. Dillan and Bob were next. Walking through and disappearing.

Genevieve, John, and Carol stood side by side, watching as the others stepped into the veil of magic. Then one by one, the girls crossed. Kate glancing back the longest, hand raised in farewell.

Then they were gone.

The wind swept across the meadow.

The three who remained turned back toward the forest. The creatures flanked them in silent procession, guiding them safely from the clearing. Piper flew high and darted in and out of the creatures.

Beyond the veil of the portal, the girls stepped into the unknown.